A POLAR EXPEDITION:

AND OTHER STIMULATING RESEARCH OPPORTUNITIES

KASS OSHIRE

Book Cover by PhantomDame

Illustrations by PhantomDame

1st edition 2023

For the books and authors who:
saved us all during the darkest of times
made us who we are
motivate us to be who we can become.

Content Advisory

THIS WORK CONTAINS: TRAUMATIC brain injury, including amnesia, medical treatment/blood talk, threats and mentions of capital punishment, off-screen presumed death of a minor, non-con mating bond, shifted sex, primal play, discussion of breeding (without pregnancy), somnophilia, lies by omission, stalking, power exchange without explicit consent, references to classist society created by preferential treatment of magically gifted individuals.

This takes place in a world that is, like our own, deeply flawed, despite my attempts to cozy it up. Please take care of yourselves, friends.

Contents

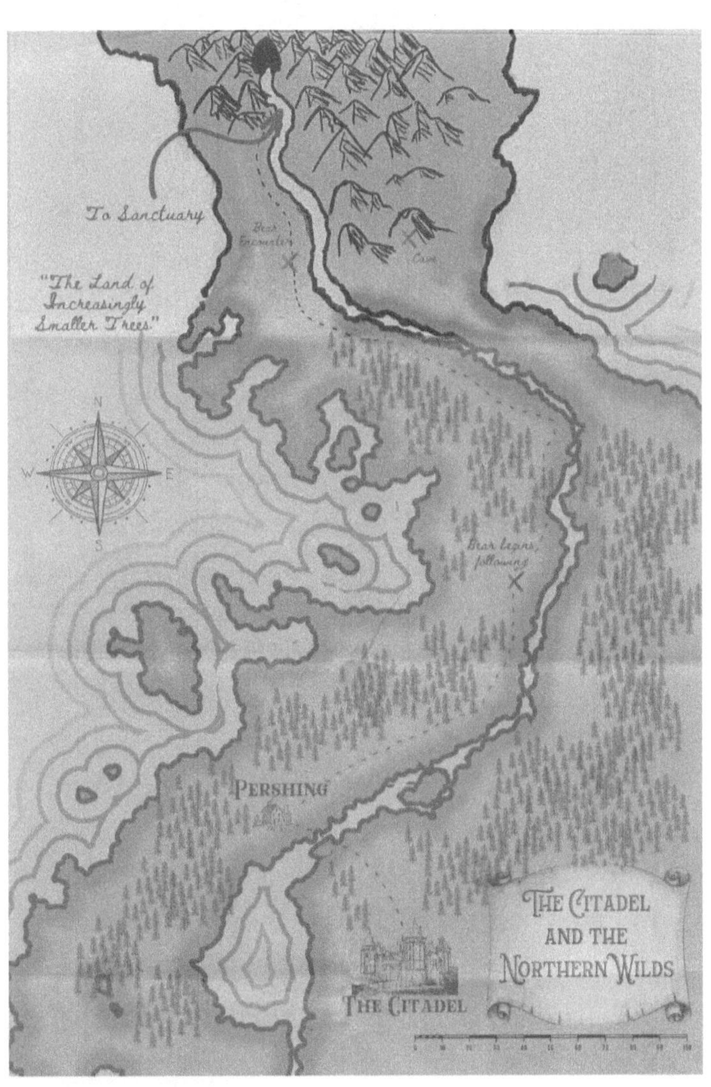

To Sanctuary
Bear Encounter
Cave
"The Land of Increasingly Smaller Trees"
N
W
E
S
Bear begins following
PERSHING
THE CITADEL
THE CITADEL AND THE NORTHERN WILDS

A Note on the Contents

THE EVENTS OF THIS work take place prior to the removal of the Lady's Barrier, specifically in the Year Post Slumber 979. My intent is to show the citizens of the Compact of Nations how others live in the rest of the world in a way that feels accessible and amusing. If you would like more concrete facts about the peoples that have long suffered under the regime of the Pathain Empire, or those of the town of Sanctuary, please see my other scholarly works or those cited in footnotes. All of the stories in the "Shades of Sanctuary " are crafted around stories told to me by those that lived them with their express consent, and any deviations from the truth are meant to entertain and have been approved by the involved parties. I will add footnotes to clarify details as needed, but my intent is that these should be treated as one might a work of fiction. Further volumes will highlight other citizens of Sanctuary, but it seemed disingenuous to not tell my own story first.

–Sirin Agbuya-Broderson YPS 1012

Chapter One

Sirin

IN WHICH SIRIN AGBUYA
IS EXPELLED FROM THE
WATCHFUL ORDER OF
LUNOLOGISTS, AND BEGINS A
PERILOUS JOURNEY, AGAINST
ALL ACCEPTED WISDOM,
ENTIRELY ALONE

AT NO POINT IN Sirin's intricate fifty-four step "Plan to Locate the Source of Magic" had she included a step for "sit in the old headmaster's office and receive dressing down."[1] Yet, there she sat nonetheless.

---

1. Steps that went unused included: Say goodbye to friends, leave a note indicating that I am headed to Meurteau, and leave at dawn, among others.

"Sirin, I am most disappointed in you. I'd thought you gave up this obsession years ago," Lord Lagrath said, wiry hands steepled in front of him, eyes and cheeks eternally drooping in disappointment.

It was simply not *possible* that this man's face was natural. Sirin studied the wrinkles on the Lord Lunologist's parchment-hued face with morbid fascination; the man looked taxidermied, frozen in time at the precise moment when he looked old enough to impart wisdom, but not yet old enough to be put out to pasture. He could claim that he didn't alter his looks magically until he was blue in the face, but no one looked exactly the same for that long without lunology.

"Our Lady provides for our magic, as she provides for the air we breathe or the water we drink. You must give up this pointless fixation. If our Goddess wanted us to know where our magic came from, it would be obvious. It is concealed from us because she wills it so." He leaned toward her, hands splayed atop the large purple-heart wood desk. "Perhaps you could research the lifecycle or temperature tolerances of lunula pyrocystis instead," he urged with a patently fake smile. As if by using the scientific term for the bioluminescent algae that fueled their magic, he could tempt her to study it rather than its provenance.

"My Lord, this *obsession,* as you call it," she spat, "is not the same as air or water at all!

We *understand* where those come from. We can observe and explain the processes required for the creation of each. We have equations and formulas detailing how they're produced, and how they interact with the world around them, and neither are finite resources. The world is covered in water and air. Doesn't it strike you as noteworthy, that lunula is only magical when it comes from the Spine? Doesn't that bear investigation? Just think of what we could do if we could make *any* strain of lunula, or even *any* algae at all, magical![2] There are places along the southern coast where lunologists have *stopped practicing* because the cost of materials is too high! And anyhow, people have researched the temperature tolerances and life cycle to *death*."

This is what happened when her colleagues were left alone. They voted their headmaster in as the leader of their professional organization so he could lord over their entire lives. Forever. For people whose magic was dedicated to changing things, they were awfully terrified of it. She had hoped in her time away some things might have changed for the better.

But no, everything was exactly as she remembered. The domed roof, the oppressive

---

2. Years of subsequent research have led me to believe that while possible, the timeframe required would be unrealistic.

feeling of darkness after sunset, the faint mildew smell clinging to his coat beside her. Dr.—no, Lord Lagrath now—had added the portraits of each graduating class from the past ten years to previously blank walls; one for each year she'd been away. Otherwise, the only addition to the room was the layers of dust built up on the bookshelves lining the walls.

Sirin's plump backside had grown over the years, but his repertoire of lectures clearly had not.[3] She could have written the entire speech down had he asked and saved them both the time and energy.[4] It seemed they were to return to their traditional roles. He would be the long-suffering schoolmaster, and she the petulant rebel railing against any authority; Sirin doubted he would ever see her as anything else.

After ten years of only brief visits between her travels, she returned to the Citadel as the last stop before beginning her expedition. Part school, part city, the Citadel was a nursery to some of the brightest minds in the world and the origin of the most important innovations of the last two centuries. There, she'd learned how to control her magic and was beaten over the head with lunula

---

3. Still has!

4. See my work of satire "How to Be the Parent or Guardian of a Happy Child."

biology, ridiculous amounts of anatomy, theory of mind, and methods for consuming large amounts of information quickly. She'd taken courses on how one could best modify their body for combat or to excel in specific professions. Endless infuriating hours were spent on the ethics of using her magic, on proper harvesting techniques, and on the entire ecosystem of the Spine River where it lived. Sirin could draw diagrams of lunula's DNA, even her own, with her eyes closed. She couldn't count the number of papers she'd written on theoretical uses of lunula, or philosophical explorations of why its use was confined to the user's body.

But the source? The all-important font upon which their magic hinged? *That* they relegated to a day-one introduction, hand-waved away as a blessing from the Goddess shared by nearly every major religion. In a place dedicated to learning, they allowed the very source of their magic to be shrouded in mysticism. Despicable. Somehow, the brightest minds in the world were content with consuming magical algae without inquiring into the advent of its existence. At every turn, professors had shooed her away, annoyed when she did not accept the same canned response.

The lack of answers wore on her like a loose tooth. The pain of the prodding was nothing compared to the satisfaction it gave her. She'd spent all of her adult life gathering whispers about the headwaters of the Spine. All she needed to do was follow it north and surely she would find the source. Find *whatever it was* that made the algae fuel their abilities. She had theories, plenty of them, and *needed* to find out if any of them were correct.[5]

"I do appreciate that the Lady has provided all she has. But she has provided what *could be* a finite resource and we have no way of knowing! If we woke up tomorrow and the river was dry, what would we do? We have no way of re-infusing it or accessing any other magic at all," Sirin declared "Are you going to tell me if that happened, you would be content to sit back and accept that the Lady had provided and she must have decided to revoke our access to magic altogether?"

"Of course not, my dear," he said. Sirin rolled her eyes again. His use of 'my dear' was her cue that now, he'd play the doting father figure to the poor little girl with no parents. Lovely. If she'd hated the routine as a girl, her ire had only grown over the years. At thirty, she'd long since lost hope he'd ever treat her as an adult, let alone an equal.

"But neither air nor water are pieces of our Lady's *soul*. The research you propose is blasphemy and may very well cost you your life. You take the gifts our lady has given us and throw

---

5. Twenty seven in fact, all of which were at least partially wrong, but twelve were at least partially right.

them in her face." He rubbed his wrinkled hand across his brow as if he had a headache before turning to her with despondent eyes. Appealing to her sense of guilt now. Right on schedule. As annoying as he was, at least he was consistent.

"I'd hoped, after you graduated, your travels would temper your zealotry with the reality of life. You have a gift, Sirin, freely given to you, and as a member of this Order, you have an obligation to use it for the betterment of society. You have a strong mind; I know that if you could find something else to fixate on, you could do such wonderful things," he droned.

Sirin sighed, relieved. If he'd reached this point in the lecture, he was winding down. Any moment now, he'd sit back down, re-steeple his fingers and dismiss her with an admonishment. She hoped her mother wasn't paying attention in the afterlife because she'd have smacked Sirin for this amount of disrespect toward her elders, but she'd passed her breaking point long ago.

He sighed, "I am afraid if we cannot come to an agreement that you will cease these efforts, I may be forced to detain you or even strip you of your membership to the Watchful Order."

What?

Sirin shot out of the chair, fists clenched at her side, body vibrating with rage. He *dared* threaten her with expulsion? Her membership in the Order was what granted her licensure to work as a lunologist. He'd beggar her if he expelled her! And for what? For daring to pursue her own research? Alone? She wasn't asking for help or permission, only peace.

She'd financed her expedition on her own, she'd planned *meticulously* for half her life, and now this antique of a man was trying to stand between her and the answers they all desperately needed. Could he truly not see that relying exclusively on one source could lead to disaster?[6] She twisted her skirt between her hands, willing her voice to calm but knowing she had only moments before she'd start shouting.

"That you would ask me to abandon finding the source of the single most important resource we have is outrageous. It's irresponsible. I am not asking to bring anyone with me. I understand the dangers of the extreme north. All I ask is that you leave me alone to do my research! If I can find the source, it could revolutionize lunology forever!" She was leaning over his desk now, her pointer finger inches from poking him in the chest.

"Sirin!" he barked, ignoring her finger as he moved to tower over her. "People have died! "He bit each word off so sharply the spittle flew from

---

6. I continue to harbor these concerns and work toward a solution, though one can easily understand why current concerns are significantly more pressing.

his lips.[7] Lowering his voice and leveling his face with hers, he reined in his temper and continued. "For years, I have tried to steer you away from this because I can't imagine losing you, too. Those deaths are our greatest shame, and my most important responsibility is to prevent more."

Sirin wasn't sure why Lord Lagrath expected this to be surprising to her. *Of course,* people had been lost trying to find the source. Everything she knew about the Arctic led her to believe it was incredibly dangerous because it was almost entirely uncharted. Disappointment settled in the pit of her stomach, while he was always infuriating, he was rarely this blatantly unimaginative. Scare tactics should really have been beneath him.

"We've lost no less than *one hundred people* on expeditions to find the source.[8] *Five* full caravans and two search parties," he said, slow and quiet.

One hundred? Seven *entire* caravans of lunologists? It couldn't be possible. She dropped back into her chair, recoiling from him as if she could escape the knowledge of such a horrific loss. Blinking rapidly, she struggled to comprehend his words, tamping down her

---

7. I still shudder at the memory.

8. 134 actually. There is a monument to them in Sanctuary, they kept meticulous records, and that's something, at least.

emotional response to the information. Could so many people truly disappear without a trace? It was unfathomable. There should've been records everywhere, whispers of lives cut short. She'd spent ten years hunting down leads. She'd have found something—wouldn't she? But, as she considered it, she recalled a few... anomalies. A lunologist that suddenly stopped publishing, or graduating classes that had seemed anemic in the reunion portraits, the explanations for absences vague.[9] There might have been a hint or two which could point toward such a thing. She'd assumed the records had been expunged for being blasphemous. Now, she wasn't so sure.

"Those expeditions were fully manned and fully armed with some of our most talented lunologists and trackers. We lost practically an entire generation of lunologists to this damn question you won't leave alone!" he snapped.

His breathing was ragged now. Sirin widened her eyes, shocked at how much this seemed to shake him. She'd never seen him so out of sorts; this was more than simply the passage of time wearing on him. He was haggard, a man worn thin from the stress of this secret. The thought of

---

9. To this day, I am shocked at how blind I was to these disappearances. I can only justify it by saying that once I decided they were anomalous, my hyperfixation on the problem dismissed any further investigation on the matter.

so many lunologists dead was nearly as baffling as the fact that so many people had already tried to find the source.

"Perhaps *someday* we could mount an expedition prepared enough to survive, but you? Alone? Sirin, it would be a death trap. We don't even know..." the Lord Lunologists cut off, voice wavering. He dropped into his chair, burying his head in his hands as his shoulders shook.

Mikail Lagrath, Lord Lunologist of the Watchful Order, the most senior member of their guild on the planet and bane of her adolescence, sounded like he might burst into tears.

"We don't even know what happened to them. They simply vanished," he whispered. "The last expedition was only supposed to ascertain the danger and return immediately, but even they were lost." He raised his gaze to hers and steadied his breathing. "I forbid you from going. You must not, under any circumstances, venture further north. Do you understand?"

Sirin blinked back at him. This was meant to scare her into abandoning her course. She'd finally worn him down and forced him to admit what he'd been hiding. What perhaps the leadership of the Citadel had been hiding for many years since they lost all of those people.

She could appreciate the Lord Lunologist's caution—she could—but this research was her *life*.

Without it, she didn't even know who she was. She couldn't just abandon it and find a new area of study. Lord Lagrath didn't understand. That was fine, no one had truly ever understood. But Sirin now knew that he, using the vast resources he possessed, would do everything he could to stop her if she persisted.

Sirin met his eyes as he raised his head. He *was* tired, and she could see his concern for her reflected in his gaze.[10]

"I understand," she whispered to him, pleased to see relief wash over his troubled face. "I didn't know. I didn't—I didn't understand."

"I know, my dear," he said. A great gust of air whooshed out of him. "I hope you understand I must swear you to secrecy. There are those who would be excited by the idea of searching for something so forbidden. If you do not hold your tongue, I am afraid I will be forced to expel you from the Watchful Order and denounce you as a lunatic." He shook his head sadly. "Every student who comes here to learn is like a child to me, and I

---

10. I speak very negatively of Lord Mikail Lagrath here, but in truth, he did more to further the advancement of society than perhaps any single person in our history. He was a champion of innovation and fostered some of the greatest minds our world has seen to adulthood. He died in YPS 1001, defending his students and wouldn't have had it any other way. May he rest in the Lady's Arms forever.

hope you know I only tell you this to keep you safe. I am sorry to break your heart so."

Sirin nodded, standing to dust off her skirts. "I'm sorry to have worried you so, Your Lordship. I understand the gravity of the situation. You don't need to worry about me any longer," she said as she moved toward the door.

"Sleep well. Tomorrow we shall see if we can pique that interest of yours in another direction," Lord Lagrath said, settling down into his chair with an exhausted smile.

"Goodbye," Sirin said, easing the door shut behind her.

The sun no longer glinted through the wavy glass windows of the halls and the gas lamps periodically spaced along the stone corridors were already lit. The lighting had always been a favorite part of her day, ever since the lines had been installed when she was a student. When she was in residence, she loved to sit on a bench in the hall, outwardly appearing as if she were studying, and watch as the maids glided between the lamps, lighting them in a routine so choreographed it seemed like a dance. Lord Lagrath had even deprived her of that small joy, having lectured her through possibly the last opportunity she'd ever have. It seemed a silly thing to be upset about, but she was too raw from the ultimatum to properly moderate her emotional responses.

If she left, she sacrificed her place amongst the Watchful Order, effectively choosing exile. There would be no support from the Citadel, no rescue party to follow her. Acquaintances at the Citadel had proven time and again that their loyalties only stretched as far as the Watchful Order sanctioned, so no one was likely to stick their neck out if she disappeared. Her family had died of a plague while she'd been a student, not even a year after she'd presented as a lunologist. She had distant relatives, but she hadn't seen them in years and only wrote sporadically, having struggled to maintain the relationships with how often she moved.

She smiled for a moment, remembering her youngest brother jumping about the room with her cousins, excitedly raving about how he would alter his body if he too turned out to be as gifted. He'd decided he would grow his muscles to be big and strong and have lightning-fast reflexes, like the heroes of old. Even if they did not share her powers, her siblings would have become sought-after partners; everyone wanted the possibility of a lunologist in the family, and they shared her genes. For a brief year, she'd drastically improved their lives and their prospects.[11] She supposed that was *something to* hold on to, to be proud of. She squeezed her eyes shut, feeling the familiar prick of pain that heralded tears.

Sirin shook her head. She needed to focus; she didn't have time for this. Opening her mind's eye, she plunged into her body, finding the trickle of lunula glowing through her veins. She could feel the warm, steady pulse of it in her heartbeat, and she dipped into it now; just a bit, right at her tear ducts. She nudged it, urging it to clamp down on them. There were many ways to accomplish this task; she could have instead altered her brain's signals or the chemical makeup present in her brain. Both felt dishonest to her, a betrayal of her family's memory. Instead, she kept the emotions caused by those chemicals, even the signals her lunula allowed her to feel sizzling along her nerves. She stopped the tears at the last possible juncture. She *didn't* have time to mourn them again, but neither would she disrespect them by wiping away her pain entirely. Her body responded to the magic's prodding instantly, stopping her tears while the stinging remained.

---

11. It must be acknowledged that pre–1001 YPS, Lunologists held an elevated status in Compact society, regardless of whether or not that elevation in status was deserved or warranted. Coming from an isolated island nation, I was eager for my family to benefit. We live in an imperfect world and I am, by no means, exempt.

What the Lord Lunologist failed to grasp was she had *nothing else.* Oh, she had casual friendships, colleagues she could rely upon to challenge her ideas when needed, and smiling faces to greet her in cities across the continent for a nice dinner and a quick liaison. She had aunties and uncles to write to, but she doubted they really knew who she was or what she was like anymore since she couldn't bear to visit and see the empty house where she'd grown up. In truth, she had nothing and no one to hold her back.

She had her work, and nothing more.

As she passed through the emptying hallways, she nodded to people she knew but she never really saw them. Sirin grimaced to herself; she knew what they would see. Silly Sirin, always seeming to not quite *fit.* Her deep brown hair would surely be escaping her braid, she'd have ink smeared across the tanned skin of her nose, her brown eyes would appear unfocused on her surroundings. The image wasn't entirely inaccurate, but it was also an image she'd cultivated. No one took her seriously, not anymore. So no one much *cared* about what she did. She hoped that meant it would be a good while before anyone noticed her missing.

Her path forward was clear. When confronted with the end of her life, professionally and literally, Sirin found she was still driven to search for her answers. If that was the cost, she was willing to pay it.

Ducking into her room, she pulled her travel pack from the wardrobe and laid it on her bed. She didn't have a suite of apartments as other lunologists who lived at the Citadel full time might have, but she'd inhabited this room each time she'd stayed at the Citadel for a visit and it was allocated for her use alone.

Smiling sadly, she looked around the room at all the small touches she'd made to make it feel more like home. Vibrant tapestries woven in the intricate geometric designs of her homeland covered the stone walls and diffusers scented the room with mango and calamansi oils. Nearly every surface was littered with the small artifacts she'd gathered in her travels. Her living wagon was much too small for much clutter, so she'd kept such things here, the only permanent residence she had.

Sirin lingered over the collection of treasures she'd accumulated over the years, filling her shelves between books. She had a small model of a theoretical vehicle, powered by lunula instead of steam, created by a friend from Meurteau. Its tiny gears and the shine of lunula from its holding tank had always brought a smile to her face, even if the design had been a failure in the end. There were carved figurines of mythical creatures, her own fantastical menagerie symbolizing the folklore of each place she'd stayed. She ran her fingers over a fierce-looking dragon who she'd positioned to breathe fire over a snarling orc. A great man-bear hybrid stood roaring on its hind legs, a myth from Pershing, the Northernmost town on the continent. Sirin smiled and pocketed it, thinking she might even check in on the little old lady who had told her such a tale when she gathered supplies there in a few days.

Picking up a small porcelain toilet, she chuckled. *That* particular invention had spread far and fast. The first time her friend had spoken of it had been with such fervor. It'd seemed too good to be true. No more covering excrement in sawdust or using latrines a hike away to hide the stench. She set it back on the shelf, sad to leave the toilet behind but spending a bit of lunula to ensure the memory stayed fresh.

And books. So many books. Children's books from home, stories about people who looked like her, in a place that felt familiar and had kept her company when she felt alone. She brushed her fingers across the spine, grateful she had the tales of foolish men with coconuts and boys who turned into stone tucked safely away in her mind. The shelves housed rare copies of works that held the hints which had sent her on her path of discovery. There was an entire shelf dedicated to books on manners from different countries of the world, which had eased her way into foreign spaces during her travels. They would, she realized, stay here; a museum of her life.

Until this evening, she'd assumed she would go, gather research for a few months, and then return home to the Citadel to write a paper on her findings. Or she would go off on another trip to chase down a colleague or a lead. Perhaps, she'd imagined, she would decide to settle near the source once it was located, but such a possibility had always assumed she would first return home triumphant. She'd share her findings and potentially invite others to join her before she settled there. Now, none of that was guaranteed or even likely.

With it went her secret hopes of a partner. Sirin had harbored the dream that if only she were vindicated, one of her casual acquaintances might take her seriously and a relationship might blossom into something beyond the casual assignations to which she'd grown accustomed. Perhaps had she stayed in one place, had she known anyone who wasn't a lunologist, she might have had a chance at something real. Instead, she'd focused on her work to the exclusion of all else, and now, it appeared it would stay that way.

Perhaps I'll tame a gaggle of Arctic animals and start a herd. I suppose I have been on the path to eccentric hermit-lady for years anyhow, I might as well embrace it. Whatever happens, happens. Though it stung to realize, more than she wanted to admit, she'd been raised to deal with the hand life dealt her, so there was no use fretting over it.

After several hours of packing, re-checking her supplies, and ensuring the waterproof coverings were secure on all the books she'd bring, Sirin crept out of the building under cover of night.[12] The massive castle that was the Citadel was cold and dark. The gas lamps no longer lit the corridors with a cheery light, a sign even the staff were asleep. Sirin used some of her lunula to enhance her eyesight, ensuring she wouldn't need to dig her lantern out of her pack. When she was a girl, she'd been no stranger to midnight creeps through these halls, but she no longer had the paths memorized, the Citadel changed so rapidly that even her mental maps couldn't keep up. She was a grown woman, and no one would normally question her moving about late at night, but it *was* decidedly abnormal for her to carry a gargantuan traveling pack through the halls. Anticipation bubbled inside of her, making her stomach flip-flop wildly.

Eventually, she made her way to the carriage house, where her horses waited alongside her living wagon. Butter's creamy coat stood out against

---

12. An updated list of recommended supplies is available in my non-fiction work "Traversing the Arctic: Tips and Tricks for Warm Weather Folks."

her brother Biscuit's, which is what had initially drawn Sirin to the pair. They were a stocky, hearty breed with thick necks and a pronounced darker stripe down the center of their manes. They'd no longer get adorable patterns clipped into them, but they'd been foaled at the Citadel, so they'd receive the best care regardless. As she approached, Butter lowered her head to sniff Sirin's hair, and Biscuit, as per usual, cracked open an eye, annoyed to be roused from sleep. Sirin giggled, the familiar feeling grounding her before the giggle caught in her throat, constricting it into a muffled sob.

There was no way they could come on this journey. It would simply be too cold, and she refused to expose them to the increasingly likely probability of death.

Tears streaming down her cheeks, Sirin pulled a few sugar cubes from her pocket for Biscuit and kissed Butter's warm muzzle. She'd been saying goodbye to them for weeks and had been breaking down into sobs anytime she thought of leaving them. "A beautiful, well-trained team like you is a treasure. They'll take good care of you, my lovelies. I promise I'll try to come back for you." She choked out, her throat constricting as she tore herself away from them toward her wagon.

She unlocked the door to her living wagon and snuck inside. The tight confines had never bothered Sirin, and she'd always appreciated the ability to move her home wherever she needed to be. Having no family to speak of had left her with a preference for drifting from place to place, following the winds of her research wherever they might lead. Without her horses, there was no way she could bring her small home. Instead, she removed the small sledge she'd purchased for her excursion and loaded it up with her pack and a few small mementos she couldn't bear to be without. A small bottle of her father's favorite cologne, which she used as a pomander when she needed to settle her nerves, A book of silhouettes with a page for each member of her family, and her prayer beads. She'd never been particularly religious, but they were small, light, and *felt* like home.

Sirin stepped out and added her things to the sledge. It looked shockingly empty, but she would purchase the bulk of her supplies for the trip in Pershing. From there, she would follow the map until she crossed into the uncharted area beyond its edges.

Sirin pulled the sledge away from the wagon, its removable wheels (of which she was *quite* proud of inventing) rolling silently, and allowed herself a brief moment to press herself to Butter's warm side. She breathed the familiar sweet scent, all warm hay and earthy goodness, her chest tight with the pain of leaving them.

Sledge loaded, horses secured, Sirin ventured into the night and took one last look at the mighty Citadel, home to all known lunologists. The massive structure which had dominated her young adulthood loomed in the darkness, on a backdrop of stars. On one side, scaffolding surrounded a new wing. That was the Citadel, always growing. Sirin rubbed at her chest, surprised at the remorse building there. For eighteen years, this place had been "home," the only one she went back to visit between her travels. Every connection she had to other people had, in some way, originated behind those walls. She grieved a moment for her home, for the inevitable loss of her community of colleagues, then turned away toward her future.

W ALKING WAS NOT FUN at first—Sirin's feet were screaming by the end of each day but she didn't have time to dawdle, afraid that the someone at the Citadel would notice she'd left and that they'd sent someone after her. A few long days of hiking overland saw her to the remote town of Pershing, situated at the border of civilization. She'd camped outside its fortified walls the previous night, only entering the city at the start of business hours. Gathering supplies had taken most of the morning and she was *fairly* certain she had everything she'd need. Her last stop, she'd decided, would be a warm lunch and a beer on her way out of town; one last toast to civilization. She was growing irritated at being around so many people, she was tired of questioning if each person was going to turn her in; she wanted to head out into the open spaces that beckoned, even though it was mid-day.

She ate a hearty bowl of stew and probably the last warm bread she'd enjoy for a long time. As she finished, she wrapped a few pastries up to eat when she needed cheering and stood with a wave to the innkeeper. It took her a minute to get the ancient woman's attention as she was pinching the cheeks of a man twice her size. He towered over the other end of the bar, radiating a joy and laughter Sirin could feel wash over her. A cap covered most of his head, but the curls she could see matched his thick white beard, though he didn't strike her as old enough for it. At the innkeeper's answering wave, he turned toward Sirin, revealing vibrant blue eyes and pale cheeks flushed pink from laughter.

Sirin swayed toward him. He was beautiful. Vibrant and dynamic in a way that made her unconsciously step closer to the man, drawn in by the sheer magnitude of his presence.

Realizing what she was doing, she shook her head and stopped. No. She had a mission to complete, perhaps the most important ever, and it did not include beautiful, breathtaking men. She snapped her gaze away from his, threw several more coins than required on the counter to make up for her rudeness, and fled from the tavern. She tapped her lunula for stealth and speed, somehow knowing he'd chase her. Her mother had always liked to say that sometimes the Lady would tempt us away from important tasks to test our dedication, and she'd not falter now. If anything, a man so delicious and captivating was a sign that she was on the right path. If she was being tested like this, with a sudden attraction stronger than any she'd ever felt, it surely meant she was headed toward something tremendous—because there was *no way* an attraction that strong was anything but divine in origin.

The houses on the one small street passed in a blur, and she kept thinking she was hearing his liquid honey laugh until she passed through the fortified wall of town. She scoffed at herself, there was no way the man would feel compelled to follow her, they'd barely made eye contact. It wasn't like he was on an important mission, the Goddess wouldn't be tempting *him* away from whatever his business was.

Once she was at the edge of the forest, Sirin finally felt like she could breathe properly again. Scrambling into the trees and hitching up her sledge, she tapped additional lunula to help with the load and headed deeper into the forest. At the last moment, she looked over her shoulder for one last look at the wooden walls that protected her from temptation.

She hiked for hours, well into the night, moving as fast as she possibly could. For most of the panicked dash, she'd been tempted to turn around, and found herself making excuses, thinking of things she might have forgotten at the inn. Her wealth of mental modifications meant that instead of a vague impression of the man, she was haunted by a sequence of pristine images. Without closing her eyes, she could see every detail that she'd missed at the moment. She contemplated each curl—wondered about the pure white color of his hair, the way he'd beamed at the innkeeper as she pinched his cheeks rosy.

Each moment she spent remembering him made her more annoyed, her motions jerky as she finally stopped for the night and gathered firewood. Ten years she'd been out of school, during which time she'd met no one half as compelling, no one who *stuck* in her mind the way he seemed to.

*Of course, it had to happen now, right when I'm
on the cusp of something great,* she fumed as she
cast her kindling into a hastily made fire pit.

He was sent to tempt her. It was the only
explanation; anything else was ludicrous. Nothing
but divine intervention could make her so drawn to
him that her feet wanted to turn around and find
him hours later. Had it been anything less than her
life's work, she knew she'd have gone back hours
ago. For that matter, she knew she'd never have
made it out of the tavern. She didn't know anything
about him. She hadn't even spoken to the man. She
hadn't needed to. Some things you simply knew.

Nothing good ever came without great sacrifice,
that was the way of it, and she just needed to
persevere. Once she'd proven herself, thoughts of
him would drain from her mind and confirm her
suspicions. She huddled next to her pitiful fire, her
face set in a determined frown. She *would* prove
her dedication to the Lady—gorgeous strangers
and dreams of domestic happiness be damned.[13]

---

13. Alternately, Sirin of the past, she could be shoving the solution
    to all of your problems in your face.

Chapter Two

Berne

IN WHICH BERNE BRODERSON,
A BEAR ONCE CONTENT TO BE
ALONE, PONDERS HIS FUTURE
AND IS TEMPTED BY A SWEET
MORSEL

BERNE STRETCHED LONG, WIGGLING his large, furry bum as he kneaded his paws in front of him. He'd been walking for hours now, easier as a bear, to be sure, but even his bear bones were tired from a twelve-hour patrol. The long day had paid off, he'd reached the end of his patrol area and was finally able to head for home.

Each time he returned, it seemed his nieces would have some new skill or trick to show him. At three, the twins changed faster than he'd have ever thought possible and he worried he was missing important parts of their lives. He still enjoyed the freedom granted by his long-ranging job, but he was beginning to think it was time to be home more. He'd been avoiding the issue, he knew, because spending more time at home also meant more evenings at home, alone.

He was a bear, so he loved being alone. He *valued* his solitude, but each night he slept in his bed, the one he'd bought with a mate in mind, was longer than the last. As he lay awake, he'd stare at the ceiling, at the unfinished loft he'd added to become bedrooms for cubs, and worry about where he'd gone wrong.

Several years ago, when he'd built his cabin, it'd all seemed so far in the future, his theoretical mate and children. Now, the years weighed heavily in his bones, and he could feel his options dwindling. He wondered why he couldn't seem to find them—or, for that matter, if he ever would; perhaps his role as pseudo-father to his sister's children was the closest he would get. So, maybe it was better if he kept to the long route. He never worried about being alone when he was curled up in a cave.

He wanted to be home.

He dreaded being home.

A push and pull he couldn't seem to escape.

Berne worried about Catrin and the girls when he was away. Worried about potential problems or catastrophes, yet he dreaded nights alone in that bed, in that empty house. He needed to make a choice, but the issue of a mate complicated everything.

Sanctuary was small, there were only so many people his age and no one seemed to fit. If he wanted a mate, he'd likely have to search abroad, as was sometimes the case. If he left, it needed to be soon. As the girls aged and came into their strength, Cat would need him around more. Problem was, he now seemed to know *exactly* what he wanted, he'd watched perfection run out of a tavern as if she'd been running for her life. The busy tavern meant he hadn't even been able to pick her scent from the rest, and he'd been detained so long by the innkeeper that by the time he left, no one in the area had seen anyone matching her description. All he had to find her was a memory of wide brown eyes and a moment's impression.

His time of waffling was slipping away; Berne needed to make some choices, and soon. He was a patient and practical bear, though. He *knew* he needed to at least go home before trying to find her. People would need to know he'd be gone, he couldn't just disappear. After he went home, he'd go after her. He didn't have any real idea as to how he would *find* her, but he also believed that the Lady wouldn't give him such a strong pull towards someone and then drop the matter entirely. The situation would resolve itself, he'd find her, sooner or later, he just needed to wait until it became clear.

Until then, he thought, *it's time for a tasty meal and an even better snooze.*

Berne sniffed the air for something to eat and let his nose lead him to a rabbit. He had a store of rations in his closest cave, but his stomach growled at the thought of a fresh meal. It was the dog days of summer, and while it was chilly, there wasn't a layer of snow cover like there was closer to the pole. The air was fresh, and flowers littered the forest floor where the sun peeked through the trees. Soon, perhaps in the morning, he would turn back toward home. The smell of the rabbit beckoned him, and he followed it through the forest toward his Lady's River.

The wind shifted, forcing him to sift through other scents to find the rabbit on the breeze. Berne dismissed the signatures of a vixen and her kit, of a snow leopard, and the myriad of flowers nearby. In short order, Berne found the rabbit, but he also found—*was that, leather?* He isolated the smell and realized it wasn't just leather, it was leather wrapped in mint and lemon, and beneath was the warm, alluring scent of a woman.

Berne huffed the scent out of his nose, confused. The closest human civilization was at least a week away, and it had been *years* since he'd encountered anyone other than his fellow rangers in these woods. He lowered his massive form to the ground, trying to be as small as possible. "Polar bear" wasn't anyone's top choice of form for sneaking, but considering his choices were polar bear or naked human, he didn't bother shifting.[1] If there was danger, he'd need his teeth and claws. If there was not, there was no point in scaring the poor lass. He was heavy and large, and this far south, he didn't even have snow to camouflage him. In his estimation, years of practice at sneaking had left him passable at best.

And sure, the question is, what is she doing out here alone? It's not safe this far north.[2] Perhaps she was lost and had been wandering the wilderness alone for weeks. Maybe she'd been separated from her group and thought herself doomed to die alone in the cold, unforgiving taiga.

What if I saved her? The thought flashed through his mind like lightning. He could shift back and help her get her bearings, send her

---

1. I am still in awe of this process. The energy expenditure and weight differential between forms defies whatever math and logic I attempt to throw at the problem, my current thesis is that lunula enables the mass to be converted to energy and stored somehow in the smaller form. I have yet to isolate where said energy is stored, however.

2. To this day, Berne and I disagree about my trip. He maintains that the Lady would have brought us together regardless without me endangering myself and that I shouldn't have gone alone, but I don't subscribe to the idea of fated mates as he does and will be forever grateful that I did.

along in the correct direction even. Poor lass was probably distraught, starving, and cold. It would be nice to save someone instead of killing them, for once. Berne quickened his pace, moving with ease, buoyed by the possibility.

He'd killed interlopers before, but it had always been born of necessity and inevitably left him with a poor appetite for weeks. All of his previous kills had been overtly hostile toward him or his people, and every one of them had worn the uniform of a scout in the Pathian army.

The Pathians were known to be relentless colonizers, the natural enemies of the Lady and, by extension, his people. They'd been prowling through his woods, searching for a land bridge to the eastern continent a few years back. Berne and his fellow rangers had dispatched at least fifteen violent Pathian scouts, four by his own hand. The people of the Compact of Nations, which made up the eastern continent, would never know they'd been in danger. As it should be. He hadn't thought twice about ripping out the throats of the aggressors and had slept well afterward. After several years of persistently sending scout pair after scout pair to their deaths, the Pathians had seemed to give up, leaving Berne and his compatriots to peace.

While he'd never quibbled about defending his home and his people's sacred charge, he'd savored the last few years of quiet. Even knowing he'd done the right thing in targeting the Pathian scouts, Berne still wondered, at times, if those scouts had families who missed them and if he'd had any other choice.

She's gonna be so happy to see me. For once I won't feel helpless, for once I'll have choices![3]

He puffed out his chest and hurried toward her, ignoring the sticks and dirt he could feel grinding into his fur. He'd do a good deed before heading home, content in the knowledge that no one had needed to die on his watch. This would be the perfect end to his patrol; he'd have the memory of his act of kindness to keep him warm during his lonely nights.

Her smell led him through the trees, and he started when he heard a gasp followed by a squeal. It was worse than he had thought, she wasn't only lost, she was in danger.

Don't fret, lass, I'm coming!

Berne increased his pace when he heard her squawk. She was afraid! He *had* to arrive in time to help her. He huffed hurried breaths as he thundered toward the sound of her distress. As he neared, Berne ducked behind a large rock and peeked gingerly around it to assess the situation.

---

3. I'd like to assure the reader that Berne has now been through therapy for the traumatic events that gave such desperation to his need to protect me.

He'd help no one blundering in, he wanted to be sure he could get the drop on anything that might be ready to attack her. Pulling a deep breath through his nose, his heart racing in preparation, he scanned the small clearing. He couldn't smell any threats; had they moved downwind? He whipped his head to glance behind him, but there was nothing there either. He turned back toward the smell of the woman expecting to see her looking frantically around, afraid and lost.

Instead, he saw a fluffy mound on the ground. It was the woman, so bundled up and bent over as she squatted, she looked more like a little round ball of fur and leather than a person. Berne furrowed his brow.

What is she doing? Did she lose something?

She was facing away from him, so all he could see was her back. She didn't seem to be crying—he couldn't hear any sniffles—but he couldn't be certain.

As quietly as he could, he circled around to the side to get a look at her face. Abruptly, he realized that her being a woman didn't necessarily mean she *wasn't* a Pathian scout. His people had female rangers, and just because they hadn't used women in the past, didn't mean they hadn't started.

Damn, I'll have to play this real careful-like.

From the side, he couldn't see any Pathian symbols on her clothing, it was all plain leather and fur. She wore a fuzzy cap and had a set of goggles pushed onto her forehead as she squinted down at the ground. She reached inside her coat and pulled out a small notebook and a writing implement. With barely a glance to find a page, she *studied* the ground as she began to scrawl in the notebook, her eyes flicking about the forest floor. Berne craned his neck to peer at the ground, what *was* she looking at?

After a moment, she started humming to herself. *What a silly wee woman.*

Was she seriously writing about the *ground?* Berne suppressed a chuffing laugh as she began to bounce in her squat, swaying her rump from side to side as she wrote. If he hadn't been shifted, he knew he'd be chuckling. Thirty seconds into her little dance, she began to talk.

"Why yes, I would gladly come speak at your conference! No, not a bother at all! Well of course my research is very, very important, but I am, as you know, dedicated to spreading knowledge above all else!" She was speaking in the common tongue of the Compact, her voice light and airy, but false, as if she was putting on a voice. She was quiet for several minutes, scratching silently in her book, perhaps even sketching, judging by the movements of her arm.

Eventually, she scoffed and started speaking again, her voice rougher this time with scorn.

"We'll *see* what mister Lord Lunologist has to say about *this!* Just try to kick me out now, you old pigeon livered goat! Every biologist in the Compact will have your balls if you expel me now!" The woman *cackled* and switched to a quieter tone of voice, one that felt less forced.[4] Her true voice was smooth and deep and had a melody and cadence to it which washed over him with a feeling of calm and focus. "Bicodulus lagomorph with elongated tail... post axial polydactyly observed on both fore and hind limbs."

Berne shook his head; the woman was incorporating some other language now, and he didn't have even a whisper of an idea what she was on about. She continued in that quiet voice, one he felt would be perfect for reading aloud next to a fire, mumbling at times. When she was quiet for a few moments, Berne recalled he was meant to be on patrol. He swung his head from side to side, sniffing for scents on the wind to see if she was truly alone. There wasn't a whiff of any other people for as far as he could smell.

I s'pose I should introduce myself, he thought, but he was so *curious* about what she was doing. Eventually, she straightened, stretching with her

---

4. The reader can imagine, I hope, the discomfort that comes from seeing oneself through the eyes of another, and I assure you I have endeavored to meddle with Berne's thoughts as little as possible.

hands on the small of her back before she giggled and did another wiggling dance.

What on Timonde?

She seemed inordinately pleased with whatever it was she'd found. She didn't seem a bit concerned with being alone. In fact, she seemed downright exuberant as she began walking away from him.

Berne followed, keeping her at the very edge of his sight, as she went to a sledge she'd left beyond an outcropping. He watched her hook several straps to herself so she could pull the sledge. Judging by the gear piled on it, she was much stronger than he would have assumed. It should have scraped along the forest floor, but when he looked closer, he could see there were wee wheels fashioned along the underside making it glide. It seemed to be working a treat; he was impressed.

If she was lost, she wasn't completely barmy. They always told weans to follow the river, that they'd be sure to come across people eventually. Though, she was walking upriver, straight toward Sanctuary, which could be a problem. Any sort of civilization she would want to find would be downriver. After about an hour of walking, the woman began to speak again, though this time she seemed to be speaking to a squirrel.

"Oh yes, Mr. Squirrel, I *do* think it is time I thought about finding a camp for the night. I *know* the sky is darkening, but I don't like how dense these trees are here. How am I to set up my tent? We'll continue on a bit more, see if there isn't a better spot up ahead." When she found a clearing, she chatted again. "Oh yes, this will do nicely. I can put my tent just here, and the fire can go in this little hollow." By the time she got her fire blazing and pitched her tent, the sun was about to disappear below the horizon. Just then, the woman stood up, waved wildly, and called out, "Good night Mr. Sun, we will see you in the morning! Please be on time, mind, we have a long way to go—I think."

She was ridiculous.

And adorable.

And she smelled entirely delicious.

And something about her tickled his memory.

And you, yeh cabbage-head, are watching her to assess her threat level, not take her to the harvest fair.

He shook his head. What in the Lady's name was he doing, he'd found a person that he'd been drawn to. Had determined that he would find *her.* Yet here he was, his tongue hanging from his mouth like an idiot, and he could feel a purr threatening in his chest. He needed to either shift and rescue this woman or decide she was a threat and be rid of her, she jeopardized his future in too many ways to count.

Problem was, she didn't seem like she needed rescuing and she didn't *feel* like a threat.

She'd set up her camp with practiced movements and didn't seem distressed at all, though from where he was positioned, he mostly saw the back of her. As the fire got going, she peeled off her outer layers, revealing a thick woolen sweater and canvas pants. From her pack, she pulled a long skirt and wrapped it around herself, settling her hands on her hips and nodding. Her large furry cap and eyewear went next, a long dark braid falling over her shoulder. A few strands of her hair had escaped and were plastered to the side of her face with sweat. Her face and neck were a warm golden tan, though now he'd crept closer, he could see flashes of slightly lighter skin at her cuffs. He could tell that while she'd clearly tried to prepare for the trip, her furs were limp and sodden in several places, evidence they weren't properly waterproofed. It was a relatively warm day, so it didn't seem to bother her, but she would be in trouble quickly if she continued north. Otherwise, she seemed quite capable. Not at all what he would expect of a woman lost and alone.

Night descended fully, and since the fire's light would blind her sight of the forest, Berne crept closer. Perhaps he could get a look into her wee book and determine if she had nefarious intent. He moved closer and saw she had wide, dark eyes which made her look suspiciously innocent, a gaze that looked shockingly familiar, that had haunted him in dreams for a week. It was *her*, the woman from the tavern, but where was the rest of her party? There was no way she was out here without a group, right?

What are yeh doing out here, lass? Should be tucked up snug somewhere, not out here alone.

The woman fetched a collapsible stool from her sledge and began to cook her supper, pulling dried ingredients from her pack and adding fresh herbs he imagined she'd picked from the local flora. It wasn't long before delicious aromas were wafting toward him on the breeze, overpowering her scent.

The smell made his stomach growl with hunger and he frowned down at it. He *needed* to be quiet or she would hear him; if she found out about him before he'd determined what to do with her he…well he wasn't sure what would happen, but he didn't want to find out.

A second after his stomach growled, the woman froze, her eyes darting to the surrounding forest. She couldn't see him, of course, but he heard her whimper.

Well fuck Berne, now you've stepped in it.

He backed away as slowly as he could, but he froze as he stepped on a branch, wincing at the loud snap.[5] He could see her chest heaving even from a distance and smell the anxiety in her scent.

Swiftly turning around, he fled as quickly as he could while maintaining a level of stealth. He didn't want her to be afraid, just needed to figure out her intentions. Once he could barely detect her scent, he paused, his chest heaved and his heart pounded in the dark.

He turned back from where he'd come, deciding that the best he could do was shift and go introduce himself. He was barely two steps toward her before he realized how startling seeing a naked man come tromping out of the woods would be. He stopped. His closest cave was at least two hours away now, and he didn't want to risk losing her by going back to find himself some clothes. With as spooked as she seemed, she might run and then he would have to track her again. He could do it easily, but he considered that would seem *even creepier* when he caught up. That wasn't even touching on how he'd smelled a snow leopard nearby and seen grizzly scat as they walked. Anything could happen to her in the four hours it would take him to retrieve clothes.

His only other option was worse, a partial shift between a man and a bear which would surely

---

5. All these years later, Berne still waggles his eyebrows at me the second he hears a twig snapping.

make her soil herself. No, he would stay close by, as a bear, which seemed the least threatening option somehow, so he could watch out for her. Hopefully, she would dismiss the sound and calm down in a moment.

She did not, in fact, calm down. All night.[6]

Berne spent the night nearby, the sharp scent of her fear on the breeze. He paid special care to be silent, so her alarm confused him. She couldn't possibly know he was still close, but she remained afraid. Easy to spook, he supposed.

As the night wore on, he crept closer when the scent of her fear lessened. Each of his steps brought him closer, and he halted when her aroma changed to enticing notes of arousal. He rumbled, low and deep in his chest, and couldn't stop himself from nearly entering her clearing. She huddled next to the fire, tent abandoned, clutching a sheathed knife as she squirmed on the ground. Her breathing was labored and he had trouble interpreting her confusing bouquet of feelings and sounds.

Should I leave? I should leave. She's asleep, but this is private.

He turned to go and the scent of her pure terror washed over him as she startled awake.

---

6. Please let's remember that as far as I was concerned there was a very dangerous predator stalking me.

He froze. He hadn't even made a noise, not a *sound,* so he wasn't sure what had woken her. Berne hated feeling trapped, and that's exactly what he was. He couldn't show himself to her, but he couldn't leave, couldn't even let her know he was there to keep her safe. As silently as he could, he backed away and eventually allowed himself to sleep. If she was determined to stay up all night, at least one of them needed to be sharp during the day and he'd be able to hear anything approaching anyhow.

The explorer writhed on the ground, her arousal wafting toward him like a siren's song. Berne swayed toward her, momentarily confused why he was a bear. He wanted to touch her, taste her, savor her intoxicating scent as it danced along his tongue. Those things required his man's body—surely. Suddenly he was upon her, still a bear, and her round little face was inches from his own. She gasped and opened her eyes, deep pools of molten desire in which he could easily drown. She smiled up at him, a glint of mischief in her eyes before she was pulled away from him, fading into the distance. He ran toward her, but he could never quite reach her, never managed to taste her sweet arousal, and he wondered if he was doomed to chase after her forever.

In the morning, she hastily packed her camp and practically *ran* upriver. He followed at a distance but couldn't believe how fast she moved. She traveled nearly as far as he would have been able to on two legs, but she pulled that massive sledge the whole time, a feat he'd never have guessed she would be able to do. Her fear scent stayed strong throughout the day, but he didn't dare leave her. She was moving farther away from his closest cave and plowing headlong toward Sanctuary.

Berne still had no idea what she was researching, and she didn't speak to herself any longer, as he'd hoped she would, so he didn't get any additional information. She didn't stop to draw any tracks again, but a few times she lingered over some and made a frustrated sound before stomping away. When he passed, he tried to see what was so interesting about the tracks, but to him they looked like regular old prints.

Near the end of the day, the woman left her gear in what he guessed would be her camp for the night and walked over to the river. It was eternal twilight this time of year and in the water, the lunula was glowing faintly. Small trickles of light played in the waters as they rushed by. Berne crept through the forest and reared up onto a tree to watch from a distance.

The explorer removed a cloth from her coat pocket and knelt to dip it into the cool waters of the Spine. It wasn't hot, by any means, but he'd have been sweaty after a day's hike like that if he wasn't in his bear form, so he imagined she'd be the same. Berne watched her from a distance as she removed her outwear, unbuttoned her shirt, and dabbed at her chest.

Berne's breathing quickened, huffing in and out in a ragged staccato. He leaned into the tree, as a breeze carried the scent of her skin to him. This was *her*, unadulterated by leather or cloth, and deepened by the day's exertion. Her shirt fell to reveal a smooth golden shoulder and his mouth watered. She was delectable, round in all the right ways, he salivated and *longed* to sink his teeth into her. She was everything he could ask for, at least as far as he knew, in a mate.[7]

A mate? How did I get to the point of mating her already? She's trespassing! And, he reminded himself with a growl, *how am I to explain that away to the council? It would be better if I could steer her in another direction, court her away from the village and introduce her without any complications.*

He dug his claws into the bark of the tree in frustration, how was he meant to turn her from her course? The woman froze, her head snapping to the side. Surely she hadn't heard him growl, or his scratch. He was too far away, too quiet.

---

7. My memory of this event is very different and I collapsed into giggles upon hearing what a pivotal moment it was for him.

She certainly acted like she'd heard him though. The woman grumbled in frustration as she wrung out her cloth and called out to the surrounding woods.

"If you are going to eat me, please kindly get on with it! This is torture and this level of sustained stress hormones is unhealthy." She looked around and Berne ducked behind the tree before she continued. "Hello? Please, just eat me and be done with it! If you're not going to, then please mind your own business!"

Well, it was not like he could "go mind his own business," as *she* was currently his business. Instead, he settled on making a small noise he hoped sounded pathetic, or at least not threatening. It was a moan of frustration.

Upon hearing it, she threw her cloth in the river and screamed out her frustration. He growled his own right back at her, causing her to freeze. Screaming like a hoyden was reckless, which he was starting to worry was a theme with her. He shook his head and ambled back to make sure her camp was ringed in his scent. Once he found an area where he could see her camp as well as the river, he relaxed, laying his head on his paws as he stretched out to wait for her to return.

Before too long, she'd made camp, eaten dinner and spent more time with her wee book. As she stood to turn toward her tent, she called out again.

"I am going to sleep now. It would be a great time for any monsters or whatever to eat me if that is their plan!" she announced. She waved her arms around for a few moments before she gave up and ducked inside her tent.

Berne scoffed. He wasn't a monster, or at least not in personality, he supposed she *might* classify him as a monster depending on his form. Not that he was anywhere *near* as monstrous as *some* he knew. He wasn't about to kill her in cold blood though; he needed evidence, one way or the other, and he was content to wait for it. He settled down with his muzzle back on his paws. He would get some sleep and stay close to her. Tomorrow he would figure out her motives, tomorrow he would know what she was up to. He would have the situation dealt with and be home by the end of the week. Then he could find her again and court her correctly, bringing her back to the village in a way that wouldn't get her killed. Wiggling himself into a more comfortable position, he fell asleep, content that he had a plan that would work to both keep her safe and win her hand.

Chapter Three

Sirin

IN WHICH OUR HEROINE
FALLS HEAD OVER HEELS UPON
SEEING THE OBJECT OF HER
DESIRE

I T TURNED OUT, TINTED goggles could only do so
much. Sirin rubbed her hand over her tired
eyes, willing even a single cloud to give her respite.
She'd thought, growing up in a tropical location,
she'd experienced a sunny day. But now, standing in
a field of snow reflecting every ray, she discovered
she was wrong. Apparently, a sunny day was biting
cold and stinging wind and squinting for so long
your cheeks hurt. The sun hung annoyingly low in
the sky, so that it seemed to always be in her eyes,

and it only set for a few hours each night.[1] Months of groundwork and years of living in a northern climate had not prepared her for the true reality of her expedition.

She'd done her research and bought or made every supply she could imagine would be needed, but truly nothing could have drilled the sheer nature of the extreme north into her. She'd been walking uphill for hours. The mountain seemed endless, and Sirin despaired of ever reaching the top. Large evergreens obscured her view, so she hadn't the faintest idea how close she might be to the summit. The trees were bowed over with heavy swaths of snow, which she knew from unpleasant experience would tumble down onto her head if she veered too close or walked too heavily.

Sirin tugged her hood lower to block the sun and did a quick check of her body. She'd learned early on having complete control over one's bodily processes was significantly more nuanced than one might assume. First, she checked her bladder levels; increasing her blood pressure to conserve heat always made her feel like she needed to urinate, so she'd turned off those nerves hours

---

1. The pole is characterized by seasons-long day or night cycles due to the axial tilt of the planet. Night in the arctic begins after the autumnal equinox and the sun is not seen again until after the spring equinox. During the time of year of my travels, the sun only sets briefly each day, and stays low on the horizon, and the majority of the day seems like dawn or dusk.

ago. The last thing she wanted was to piss herself because she wasn't monitoring it carefully.[2]

While she'd packed for the weather, even these late summer temperatures were colder than she'd ever expected. The balance between the amount of heat her muscles produced, the calories she needed to consume to make heat, how much she allowed herself to sweat, and the amount of lunula she needed to consume to manage all of it was *exhausting*. She nodded to herself; her bladder could make it a while longer. Her internal stores of lunula seemed sufficient, but she *could* use a snack. Her body was getting close to tapping the fat stores she'd carefully cultivated for heat retention and she'd worked too hard to lose them now.

Looking up at the sky, Sirin could see she had a few hours left of the day. With zero reference points, she doubted her map would be of much use, but she felt she needed to see it anyhow. For motivational purposes.

Sirin paused for a moment, took off her large pack, and slipped her water skin from its spot next to her chest. The water inside was tepid

---

2. It should be noted that only experienced lunologists should tamper with their natural bodily processes in this way. It is imperative that novice lunologists train under supervision. If you or someone you love are looking for assistance with learning to use lunula safely, please contact your local chapter of the Egan Ghanim Foundation to access a network of surviving lunologists.

at best, but it felt startlingly warmer than the frigid air she'd been breathing. She drank deeply and then searched for her notebook, flipping to a page depicting an intricate map. Consulting her compass, she made what few notations she could.

Sirin traced her progress beyond the end of the existing map, drawing a few more trees and labeling this "the land of progressively shorter trees." She'd hoped she would find an *actual* landmark soon so she could add a real marker. She folded it up and prepared to push ahead. The trees were thinning, and she worried soon the never-ending landscape of green, brown and blinding white would be reduced to a squint-inducing monochrome. She would likely go mad if that happened. The thought of being surrounded by *nothing* but the snow made her shiver; surely she would find the source of the River Spine and the lunula before then.

Sirin pulled out her notebook and inhaled deeply, filling her lungs and scenting the air, verifying she was still being followed. Among the crisp forest scents, she could still detect *him*.

She'd become so habituated to the deep musk of the bear that she had to actively search for it, her amplified sense of smell allowing her to filter the bear's specific pheromones from the myriad of other animals in the area. At this point, his scent was like air or trees—expected. A week ago, though, Sirin had spent the entire first night after scenting him without sleeping, clutching her knife, and cursing herself for not bringing one of those explosive flintlock things.

Over the week the bear had dogged her, her fear had slowly faded to curiosity. Now, she idly imagined them to be traveling companions, two lonely souls in the unforgiving taiga, happy to have found companionship. He likely lived in the area, she reasoned. He *was* a bear. Judging by his footprints she figured he was a grizzly, though she'd been fairly certain they didn't range this far north; she hadn't expected or planned for any bears at all, since there was so little documentation about arctic fauna. Sirin had heard myths and whispers of fantastical creatures living this far north, likely bears were not exciting enough in comparison. She'd seen only hints at such fabled creatures; rabbit tracks with multiple tails, or a cat screech which seemed to come from the sky, but even those tidbits were wildly exciting, so she did a happy wiggle just thinking about it.

Her bear, however, seemed decidedly mundane, apart from his fascination with her, of course. The past two days, she'd begun leaving him bits of jerky, in hopes he would not see her as a threat.

Alternatively, he could decide I am tasty, just like jerky, she reminded herself. Sirin made a few notations in her notebook and drew a small doodle of a bear wearing a suit bowing in the margin. She giggled at the thought of the bear using the stiff formal introductions required when there was no one else to do the introduction.

"Hello, madam, I would make myself known to you," she said aloud, cutting a bow and giggling to herself. He would swipe off his smart little cap and she would offer him a cup of tea. They could discuss their mutual quest and laugh over some jerky.

Silliness, I am a goose, she thought. She'd always had a penchant for talking to herself and fostered a lively imagination, but perhaps the weeks of solitude were scrambling her mind. Before the bear, she'd had only her musings and mounting kinship with the lost adventurers to keep her company. A shared purpose that had kept her company or helped her stay focused when she was plagued by thoughts of the man from the tavern.

Sirin blushed, thinking about the other ways her mind seemed to be scrambled. Only hours after scenting the bear for the first time, she'd begun having strange dreams. Dreams during which the bear chased her relentlessly through the forest. Dreams where she felt absolutely terrified of being caught. But also, dreams where, when she *was* caught, she'd been ravished by that man from the tavern.[3] She'd then wake in the night, breathless and panting, mid-orgasm and disoriented.

No, the last thing she needed was to think too hard on *him* now. If she let herself dwell on her dreams, she'd only have to waste even more energy and lunula on tamping down her arousal, and so far today, she'd been managing quite well, she'd only needed to do it twice. Somehow, her fear from the bear had triggered some sort of pathetic instinct that, she assumed, wanted her to seek protection. Well, her subconscious would just have to accept there *was* no handsome stranger around to save her from the bear, and she didn't seem to need saving anyhow.

Her brief respite over, Sirin continued her plod through the snow for the next hour, at which point the trees began to peter out. She could see the land transitioning to some sort of ridge or cliff ahead. The sun was getting low in the sky, so she might as well trek up and take a look over top before camping for the night. If she was going to need to do some repelling in the morning, she wanted time to prep tonight.

She breathed deeply, at peace as she left the trees behind her, feeling like she was on the cusp of something extraordinary. She realized, as she let out her breath, she could no longer scent her bear.

She diverted a measure of her internal lunula reserves toward increasing her sense of smell further and she could barely detect him, but instead of behind her, he was ahead. She enhanced her vision for distance, squinting to block out the additional light, and didn't even have time to properly register that change when a massive white bear crested the hill. Sirin froze, her heart beating rapidly in her chest. Her lunula allowed her to feel her body's natural responses to fear, the release of adrenaline overpowering her annoyingly ever-present arousal. It poured out of her adrenal glands into her bloodstream and rushed through her in a tide, making her heart beat faster, her breathing quicken, her muscles twitch, and even her digestion slow as resources were shunted away. This awareness allowed her to remain calm, despite the terror that pulsed through her.

She nodded toward the great bear and began to walk slowly back toward the trees. She figured she had twenty yards until the tree line and then she would probably turn and run. Sirin might like to think she was friends with the bear in her head, but this was a wild animal. With barely a thought, she enhanced her eyesight so that she could catalogue this strange, potentially new species of bear's behavior.

What were you supposed to do if you saw a bear again? There were different rules for brown and black bears, she knew, or was at least able to pull from one of the trail guides she'd memorized, but this bear was neither. He chuffed at her, herding her toward the tree line with great plodding steps.

He stood in her path, blocking the most direct route to the rise, and glared down at her. She'd never before seen a bear in real life, but she was sure it seemed entirely too *aware* for her tastes. He sniffed the air and then shook his head as if trying to clear out a scent and then trained his eyes back on her. Sirin stood, frozen, she'd never even heard of what to do with a white bear, perhaps it was an albino grizzly?[4] Surely she could remember what to do when encountering a grizzly. Oh, she'd read it but the adrenaline was interfering with her ability to *find* it. She shunted a fair bit of her lunula reserves toward processing speed and reaction time, keeping a bit back for last–second modifications. Around her, the world seemed to slow, giving her the time she needed to find the source.

She didn't like what her faster brain told her. He was not acting similarly to any of the three prior bear encounter accounts she'd read. She did find a passage from a survival text which said if the bear was stationary to walk slowly sideways and back away from the bear. She angled her body away and gently stepped farther down the mountain. Each time Sirin retreated, the bear seemed to nod its head and amble closer to her. It let out another

---

4. Berne's shifted form is ursus maritimus, now commonly known as a polar bear.

chuffing noise before rearing onto its hind legs and waving its large paws at her.

This could not be normal behavior. Bears don't herd people down mountainsides, but that was exactly what he is doing. Perhaps he was rabid, didn't animals do strange things when rabid? The farther she went, the more she realized it to be true. This massive bear *was* shepherding her down the mountain, directly away from where she needed to go.

They locked eyes as she retreated. With her enhanced eyesight, it was like he was only feet away from her. His eyes were entirely too deep, too intelligent. Not that she'd ever seen another bear to have any frame of reference at all, but she'd never seen this amount of clear thought on an animal before. Sirin was terrified to look away from those soulful eyes; some part of her knew, if she broke his gaze, she was done for.

Sirin sped up her pace, hoping she was close to the tree line. *Lady, please let me be close!* Once she was through them, she planned to break and run, augmenting her speed so he couldn't follow. She readied what lunula she had left, far less than she'd like, to pour into her muscles. Suddenly, she heard a cracking sound, just as the ground beneath her gave way and her stomach lurched as her vision flooded with blue and she felt herself falling.

Chapter Four

Berne

IN WHICH, IN ORDER TO
PROTECT THE SAFETY OF A FINE
LADY, OUR HERO STEALS HER
SHOES

T HE CURIOUS WOMAN CREPT away from him, back toward the tree line. She'd already tortured him for a week with her scent and her noises as she slept, and her closeness, and now she was going to force him to stop her. For a week he'd tried redirecting her away, but she'd continued determinedly on, strangely acting as if she was entirely nonplussed by the danger he posed. *How* could he dissuade her from continuing? How could he convince her to leave entirely? Was she *intentionally* crossing the Boundary or was it just the way she was progressing? His people,

the Shades, had maintained complete secrecy for
nearly a thousand years and he wasn't going to
be the one that endangered them or their Lady,
nor was he going to get the woman he was
increasingly sure was his mate killed because of
his carelessness. A week of wrestling with his
options hadn't gotten him anywhere.

For the entirety of the time he'd followed her, he'd
been plagued by erotic dreams of her at night, and
worries of how flippantly she careened through
life during the day. He'd often had fantasies about
dragging her back to one of his caves or his cabin
and feeding her a proper meal, rather than the
bland ones she'd eaten since he'd been following
her. During each day, she interrupted his worries
at least three times with a specific form of torture.
She'd stopped to masturbate often enough to
torture him mercilessly. For a week, he'd deluded
himself that she *wasn't* going exactly where he
thought she was, that she *wasn't* pointed like an
arrow at the very people and place he was meant
to keep her from.

As much as he'd tried to deny it, she *was*
following the river. There were things written
in her wee book and on her well folded map
which *could not* be made public in the Compact of
Nations. One hint of a hybrid creature would have
scholars flocking here. Before he could even think
of what to do though, he *had* to get her away from

the border proper of his people's territory. If she crossed, he wouldn't have any choice left at all. He'd have to turn her in and he'd no longer have a say in the matter.

He waved his arms and reared up, urging her away from the Boundary and the choices he needed to make. He didn't have the slightest idea what he would do with her once she was back within the tree line, but first, he'd get her there. He knew what he was *supposed* to do, but the thought didn't sit well. Her flushed face remained pointed at him, but her brown eyes frantically darted around the forest as she crept slowly backward..

She is, he thought, *quite good little prey, going exactly where I need her.* He feinted left, hoping to herd her a bit farther away from the river. She was nearing the first spruce, almost back in the forest. All he needed to do was to get her *away* and then he could confront his moral dilemma.

Before he could blink, before he could react, she was falling backward, toward the massive tree, feet flying over her head.

Berne froze, panicking. His heart pounded in his chest and a wave of cold swept over him. Perking his ears, he listened for any sound which might indicate if she'd survived, but he couldn't hear even a whimper of pain. She'd gasped as she fell but now it was horribly silent. He could, however, taste the sharp tang of her blood in the air. The taste or scent of human blood had never bothered him particularly, but this felt wrong. Some place deep inside of him rebelled at the idea of her hurt. She was *bleeding.*

Berne rushed over, careful to avoid the lip of the tree well she'd fallen into.[1] The branches of the spruce stopped the snow from reaching the surrounding ground, creating a deep hole with the trunk at its center. This specific well seemed to be a good bit deeper than he was tall, so he spread his body wide to not collapse the wall of snow atop her.

The tree above her hung heavy with snow. As soon as she woke and struggled, she would be buried, suffocating from the weight. The more she attempted to dig herself out, the more would fall on her. Inching closer to the edge, he peered inside. His woman had cracked her head on the trunk of the tree and her blood oozed slowly from the wound. Her hat was dislodged, her long black hair becoming matted with blood, and she was far too pale. One of her arms lay at an unnatural angle and she was uncharacteristically still.

The whole scene made bile rise in his throat. He found himself salivating and making popping

---

1. In extremely snowy areas, the branches of evergreen trees shield the ground beneath them from receiving as much snow as the surrounding area, creating an often deep well which can be extremely dangerous. When falling in, individuals can hit their head and can be suffocated under snow in efforts to rescue them.

sounds with his jaw subconsciously.[2] He shifted from foot to foot, his body wanting to *do* something.[3] Only an hour ago, she'd charmed him with her silly little voices and wonder at everything, her sudden giggles, and happy dances. She was supposed to flit wildly from each thing she found fascinating, careening here and there on a whim. And now, she lay motionless in a hole and it made him want to roar. She was a spark of light. Everything about this was wrong.

He breathed in, trying to stifle his instinctive reactions so he could think clearly. Her scent in the air was *wrong*. The entire time he'd followed her, she'd smelled of determination, curiosity, and at times, frustration and exhaustion. *This* scent, though, the faintest hint of fear, plenty of blood, and *nothing at all* was so incongruous with what he knew of her. She *never* smelled of nothing at all, even asleep, her scent had broadcast her emotions from her dreams. He shook his head, snorting the empty scent from his nose. At least he could see her

---

2. Shifters tend to exhibit signs of distress associated with their animal in both forms. All of these are signs that would seem odd in a human, but demonstrate distress in bears.

3. Over my years with the people of Sanctuary, and specifically shifters, I am constantly fascinated by the interactions between their human logic, emotions and instincts and those of their shifted form(s). While there are recommendations on how to balance the two "selves" it is still something that each shifter must navigate on their own, with varying levels of integration.

breath making small puffs in the air above her face and her airway didn't seem obstructed.

Since he'd been tracking her, he'd grown a significant respect for her determination and grit. She was a small woman, rounded and soft, yet her stamina was excellent. She'd made him laugh more than once over the last week, talking to herself, or doing a wee dance when excited. It was exceedingly foolish being out here alone, why had she not brought anyone?

If she'd not been alone she wouldn't have gotten hurt.

He growled in frustration.

Had she not been alone, they'd have never found one another.

He hated that whoever her people were hadn't stopped her because now *he* was responsible for her pain and he was responsible for stopping her. By all rights, by everything he'd been taught, he knew the council would expect to leave her there, bleeding in that hole.

But there was *something* about this lone wee woman, so bundled up she was nearly round, trudging through the wilderness, that pulled at him. His woman, while using less-than-ideal cold weather attire, had trekked for days, alone, in the deepest wilderness. This soft, plump thing could not *possibly* be a danger to them. She was strong, sure, but she posed no real threat to him or his people and he was annoyed that mere interest was viewed as dangerous. She had an exuberance about her that fascinated him and it would be a shame to have it snuffed out needlessly.

But if she was searching for the source, as it seemed she must be, she *was* jeopardizing their purpose. There was no good way out of this mess or at least one he would find when he was so distressed. If she was going to heal or wake up and try to cross the Boundary again, he shouldn't leave her. No. That would be a breach of his duties just as much as it went against his instincts.

The best thing, he thought, *would be to get her out of there and then figure a plan. I can't just leave her. I can just remind them that if I left her and she healed, she'd be in Sanctuary within a few hours.*

For the moment then, his course of action was clear. He shuffled to the downhill side of the tree and a fair bit back from the well itself. He dug in toward the mountainside; each swipe of his paw brought large swaths of snow down, and he stamped his feet to pack it firm. The most important thing, he knew, was making sure his structure was sound so when he broke through the wall of snow, he would be able to pull her out quickly. He shoveled and packed, shoveled and

---

4. This method, digging into the side of the well and creating a packed ramp is one of the safest methods for extracting someone from a tree well.

packed.[4] This process was significantly faster with a group to ferry the snow farther, but he was alone and he would simply have to be enough.

Seconds before he breached the wall of the well, Berne took a minute to rest and recall her positioning. If he could, he would grab her pack, but he refused to let it hinder him. He remembered one of her arms would be closest to him, so he'd grab her there.

Gently, disturbing as little of the tree's snow as possible, he eased his way through the last bits. Several large drifts collapsed on her and he frantically pawed the snow away until he found her arm. For a moment, he considered pulling on her clothing, but he couldn't risk it ripping. He took her forearm in his maw and gave a powerful tug. She shifted toward him, and he backed down the ramp he'd made as quickly as possible. He tried to pull at a steady pace, but he only managed lurching pulls. One arm was broken, and now the other was at least bruised, if not punctured or dislocated.

Still, he mused, *she'd rather be alive and injured than dead. And she's no wilting flower; she can take it.*

With a final heave, he saw her clear of the ramp and danger.

---

4. This method, digging into the side of the well and creating a packed ramp is one of the safest methods for extracting someone from a tree well.

For a moment, he studied her. He could barely make out what she looked like under her thick layers, but the blood from her wound seemed to be slowing. The trail of it she left behind her threatened to rile him up again.

Focus! He chided, *going roaring and stamping around isn't going to help anything. Just focus on what yeh need to do right now. Right now I need to—why is she laying all askew?*

He nosed her shoulder and spotted her pack underneath her. He chuffed, the closest he could make to a laugh in this form. *That* was why he'd had such a hard time pulling her out.

Now that she was free of the tree, he was faced with figuring out what he meant to *do* with her.

Leaving her here on the snow was no different than down in the hole, so he should at least get her to shelter. He shifted back to his human form, the familiar shrinking and itching feeling provided a small measure of grounding to his panicked mood. He immediately felt the bite of the cold snow on his bare feet and shivered. He was less sensitive to the cold in his human form than a regular human would be, but he would quickly freeze to death if he remained naked in this weather. Berne had a few minutes before he would feel the chill too badly. Berne reached down and gently turned her head away, praying she didn't wake up. The last thing he needed was her waking up and staring at his cold-shriveled cock.

Berne stood, wiping his hands on his thighs before reaching for her pack. Luckily, she had some rope secured through a strap, so he unwound it. He hefted her onto his back and looped the rope around their bodies loosely. He had *some* idea of how much slack he might need to accommodate his other form, but he knew it was a guess at best. Berne pulled an end through another loop and clutched it in his teeth. He didn't look forward to having to bite it the whole way, but it gave him some ability to size the carrying harness he'd made.

Satisfied with how secure she felt , he shifted back into his bear form, letting out a wheeze as the rope tightened uncomfortably. He shifted his weight, testing her balance on his back. It wasn't perfect. He'd need to be careful, but it was workable. He had a cave nearby, so he didn't have to carry her too far.

The makeshift sling ended up working better than he'd expected. Every so often, he would need to throw his weight one way or another to shift her back to a stable position. Nevertheless, Berne made good time, and they arrived at one of his patrol caves within an hour. He kept them tidy, so there was a firepit, a cleared-off area for her to rest, and even a door he'd fashioned to close it off.

When he settled her down, he quickly dressed in his wool tunic and pants and went to check her wounds. He cleaned and bound her head, removing her strange eyewear and brushing as much of her hair away from the gash as he could. It would need a good wash and stitching, but he didn't have any needle or gut as any cuts he had were always solved with a quick shift. His knowledge of bones was not going to be sufficient to set her broken arm, either. He would need to get help from Sanctuary if he had any hope of saving her.

In the plodding way of a bear, he'd simply done the next logical thing, one after another, and now found himself in a bit of a situation. It had all seemed so clear yesterday. Follow the strange woman, scare her away if she got too close to Sanctuary, go home and tell everyone he was leaving to find a mate, find her again, mate her and return home. If he took her to Sanctuary now, she'd be in immediate danger. So why did he suddenly feel the *need* to do just that?

His whole life, their policy had been a swift elimination of *anyone* who pressed the Boundary, but recently the council had found texts indicating the Lady might have disagreed with such practices. Until now, he hadn't much cared how they decided. Never before had he questioned his people's tenets against outsiders the way he had in the last week. He *knew* they had a sacred duty to protect; but since he'd begun following her, Berne had found himself railing against about the compulsory execution policy. If he was honest, he supposed it had never really sat right with him but she was forcing him to admit it.

Maybe it was something about her. Or, he considered, it was that she reminded him of Annika. Not in any specific way, just—she was out here, alone, with such joy and exuberance. Thinking of his baby sister made his throat tighten and he groaned in anguish, the feelings hitting him as if she'd been lost yesterday. He hadn't been able to save Nika, but maybe he could save his woman.

Perhaps that was all it was—a lingering wish that he could have done something. A fantasy that he could have known she was in trouble, could have gone to her, instead of searching for her only to find, days later, what was left. He shook his head, trying to dislodge the image of the blood spattered snow and the shreds of Annika's clothing. This woman didn't need to die, not like that. He *knew* the council would prefer he let her die, if not do the deed himself. But looking at her, he didn't see how he could. He hung his head and let out a confused moan, long and low.

Perhaps I'll leave, and when I return, she'll have fled and the problem will resolve itself, then, I can just find her again in a few weeks like I'd planned, he thought, starting to hope and then realizing the thought of being away from her now was offensive. And anyhow, the council would never allow it; if they got even the tiniest whiff or hint of her, which in a matter of days another ranger would be around and catch her scent, he'd have to hunt her down. Or worse, that other ranger would, some young buck who wouldn't even consider the new ways of thinking. She couldn't leave.

He waved his head from side to side in frustration and groaned again.

This wouldn't be a problem if she wasn't so adorable. She's too bonnie by half is the problem. He huffed, coming to a decision. *I'll just have to make sure she stays. When they meet her, she'll make 'em realize we can't go around killing perfectly normal folks for investigating things that merit investigating.* He wasn't sure what they should do *instead,* but that was why *they* were the council and *he* was just a border ranger.

He nodded to himself, his woman was the perfect example to prove things *needed* to change around here. He could pop back, and get someone *actually* knowledgeable about medical stuff and a council member to handle the situation. She'd likely lose her research, and she'd be crushed, but anyone would rather lose a bit of writing than *die.* Or, Berne considered sheepishly, *perhaps* they'd let her keep her research if she stayed. He wouldn't mind at all, she could even stay with him if she needed until they assigned her housing. The thought spawned a pleased smile—it sounded nice.

His mind entirely clear on the matter, Berne settled her close to the fire pit and built a small, contained fire. Hopefully, it would burn for nearly as long as it would take for him to get back. He pulled a few bits of jerky from her bag and left them on her chest before he took off her shoes and thick woolen socks. A warm blanket tucked around her, Berne grimaced with distaste. He didn't like trapping her here, but taking her footwear and supplies seemed the kindest way of keeping her in one spot. After double-checking the fire and her blankets, he tied both of their bags onto a bundle, shifted back to his bear, and crept out the door.

Chapter Five
Sirin

IN WHICH OUR HEROINE IS EXCEEDINGLY ANGRY AT HER OWN CONFUSION, THE PEOPLE AROUND HER, AND LIFE IN GENERAL

S IRIN WOKE TO NEAR darkness and pain. Her head throbbed and her whole *body* seemed to ache. Of all the types of pain there were, she was lucky to experience several of them at once. Joy. She blinked, wondering why her tent was so cold. Shifting to turn on her little portable stove, she hissed as pain shot through her shoulder. Immediately, she attempted to repair the area but found her lunula stores almost depleted. Had she fallen asleep without drinking more lunula, *again?* The cold seemed to increase as she slowly became aware of her surroundings. She was not in her bed at all, but in a cave. Next to her a sputtering fire provided some small measure of warmth and light. What little she could see of the cave did not seem the least bit familiar, nor did she remember camping here for the night.

How had she gotten here? Sirin tried to recall where she'd been and what she'd been doing, but her thoughts kept slipping from her mind. Last she could remember, she'd snuck out from the Citadel earlier than she'd planned. Perhaps she'd camped here for the night and somehow forgot? No, camping here for the night did not account for any of her injuries or why she didn't seem to be wearing footwear at all. She could only surmise she'd somehow injured herself and had been rescued by a group sent by the Citadel.

Dammit, this is not what I need. A wave of panic washed over her, making her feel like she'd been dunked in ice. The consequences for going against the Lord Lunologist could be dire, and she had no interest in finding out what hers might be.

Sirin turned her head, trying to see if she could get any more oriented while being completely horizontal. From her limited view, she couldn't see her pack or any other supplies the other scholars might have left. She realized she couldn't smell other humans either. Her sense of smell was heightened, but she hadn't the faintest idea why.

She could smell *something*, though. What she couldn't understand was why she was having a hard time identifying the scent. It didn't match any animal she'd ever smelled, but also, somehow, it felt familiar. It wasn't human, but it was close, and it also reminded her of a bear, her bear specifically. The scent had faded, so he wasn't here with her now, but she'd guess he'd been here recently.

It must be the scent of my human rescuer over that of a bear who lived here at one point. She sat with the thought for a minute, but it felt wrong. Except it was only one smell, and it was fresh.

I suppose it could be possible for another lunologist to change their scent.[1] *Perhaps they were trying to blend into nature and are using bear pheromones as a model. That must be it. Smart, I hadn't ever considered it, but it seems like it would be handy.*

She thought about how she might go about synthesizing bear pheromones, but she couldn't seem to recall how she'd indexed her books on pheromones. This would *not* do. How was she meant to get herself out of this situation if she couldn't even pull information out of her brain?

Sirin tapped the small amount of lunula she had left in her blood and checked her injuries. Her head

---

1. I will be honest, looking back, knowing the severity of my brain injury, I am fairly proud of this theory.

wound seemed to be mostly a concussion with a small laceration. She'd broken several bones in her left arm, but it did seem to be a single impact fracture across both, so she'd had worse. Her right forearm had sustained some bruising and several puncture wounds which might indicate an animal bite of some sort, which was odd. Her right shoulder was also dislocated, but that seemed the extent of her injuries. She spent the last bit of her lunula attempting to heal the hematoma in her brain, but she ran out before her body could repair all the damage. A body could only be pushed so far, so fast, on such a small amount of magic.[2]

With a sigh, she allowed her head to gently rest back onto her hat, which she was surprised to find under her head, cushioning it. As soon as she allowed herself to relax, Sirin felt her eyelids droop. She shook her head to keep herself awake, and spikes of pain jolted through her skull. With a groan, she allowed her eyes to shut. She knew she shouldn't sleep, concussed as she was, but the lure of rest was too strong to resist.

---

2. Second time readers are likely laughing at how narrow my definitions of the capabilities of lunula were.

S HE WOKE UP TO distant noises. Keeping her eyes closed to concentrate, she could make out several distinct footfalls and at least three voices. The conversation sounded tense, though she couldn't quite make out the words.

She shivered. The fire was completely out at this point. Hopefully, they would restart it when they arrived. She tried to match the voices to any of her colleagues, but none seemed to fit. There was one grumbly deep voice, a curt one that spoke quickly, and a high feathery voice she could barely make out.

After a few moments, their footsteps stalled, and they stopped speaking. Sirin strained to hear them but was met with only silence. Seconds passed with nary a sound and her heart rate increased.

Why aren't they coming? Have they decided its better to just be rid of me? They can't just leave me here!

Her heart sped as she considered being stranded for any significant length of time. Surely she wouldn't live long, as vulnerable as she was. She had absolutely nothing to eat, no wood for a fire, and no way of fixing that.

She pitched her voice as loud as she was able and called, "Hello? Help! I am over here! Please! I need help!"

The volume made her wince, but Sirin knew it could be her only chance at living. She quieted to listen for a response and was rewarded with the curt voice saying a few words before footsteps resumed in her direction. Sirin's throat clenched and her vision blurred with tears. A shuddering sob left her as she waited. She didn't know who these people were, but they were clearly at least curious enough to investigate, for which she was extremely grateful. She instinctively reached up to dash the tears from her eyes and groaned at the pain in her shoulder.

Outside, a deep voice called "Coming!" and the footsteps picked up as they switched to another language. It seemed odd to Sirin that she didn't recognize it. She spoke a fair few and could at least *identify* many others. The cadence sounded familiar to her, it rolled and lilted, but her head wasn't as clear as it should be yet, so she stopped trying to identify it.

They stopped speaking entirely as they approached her until the curt voice called out a heavily accented "Halloo? What's the craic? We're here to assess your injuries."

"I'm in here," Sirin called. A wave of gratitude washed over her, threatening to make her cry once more. She squinted as a tall, rangy woman with close-cropped white hair entered and rushed to kneel at Sirin's side, a lantern near blinding her after the dark. The woman's skin was deeper than Sirin's, surprising in these northern latitudes, but Sirin didn't recognize her face. There were hundreds of lunologists at the Citadel, so Sirin came to the conclusion that she just hadn't met this woman. Her clothing was a style Sirin didn't recognize either, which *was* odd. There were plenty of cultures represented in the styles of dress at the Citadel, as lunologists came from across the continent, but the *fabrics* this woman wore didn't seem made of any fiber Sirin knew either. The woman dropped a bag on the ground next to Sirin and began assessing her injuries, her eyes searching and hands lightly probing.

"I'm Arndis. I'm a healer," she said.

Ah, this is the curt voice. Arndis spoke in a way that barely tickled the edges of Sirin's knowledge, but the name of the language corresponding to the accent continued to elude her[3].

"I'm Sirin," she gasped as Arndis probed a particularly tender spot. A grumble near the entrance drew her eyes. Another woman and a

---

3. The people of Sanctuary speak Gailage, a language which shares some commonalities with several languages spoken by peoples of the Compact, though isolation has led to drift among related languages. Their accent is a rhotic, lilting brogue, characterized by several trademarks when they speak Common. They sometimes pronounce T as CH so "two" becomes "chew." TH is often voiced as T so "three" is said "tree." In words ending ING, the G is often dropped, and vowels are flattened, making "are" sound like "air." Finally, consonants at the end of words can have a softly voiced "echo vowel." Interested parties can learn more in The Language of Our Lady by Matilda Broderson.

man stood there, both paler of skin and hair than Sirin, as she might expect this far north. It surprised Sirin that the man was vaguely familiar, though surely she'd remember someone so…big? He was broad-shouldered and towered over the wisp of a woman next to him. He had solidness, a thickness to him she found quite appealing. The woman stood with her arms crossed firmly and the man with his fists clenched at his side. It struck her as odd that they all shared starkly white hair even though these other two were pale and of the three, only the woman by the door looked old enough for hair of that color.[4] Sirin trawled through her mind to see if she could place their faces but again came up blank. She *should* be able to remember someone as remarkable as that absolute beast of a man, surely?

Curse this brain injury, I should at least recognize *them, or that fabric they are wearing!* Sirin looked back at Arndis, willing her brain to remember *anything* about this woman, but nothing she wore gave Sirin any clues. The embroidery at her cuffs didn't remind Sirin of any

---

4. Another hallmark of the people of Sanctuary is the bleaching of their hair by proximity to the source. Individuals who move to the area and the F1 generation can have their hair color restored by sufficient time away. F2 and beyond have intrinsically white hair, and though lunologists can alter this, the color will fade if not maintained. Interestingly, skin color does not seem to be affected, as the people of Sanctuary have a wide array of skin tones.

culture she could remember. The cut of her shirt and trousers was unfamiliar too. Sirin wanted to *scream.*

She'd sacrificed so much, and spent all her time, lunula, and effort in building the perfect brain for research. Others had used lunula to modify their bodies, to be better at fighting, or become more graceful. But not Sirin. No, she had enhanced her mind so she could keep entire texts of books stored for reference, like a maze of bookshelves, organized as intricately as the library of the Citadel was. Her photographic memory and excellent drawing hand had only augmented her mental library. And now she couldn't even look up the provenance of a type of fabric or embroidery pattern? This horrible, sluggish thinking made her want to pull out her hair in chunks.

Arndis interrupted her mental tirade. "Ach, can yeh tell me how yeh feel?"

"Oh, I have a concussion with a small hematoma, a fracture on both my ulna and radium in my left arm, and the other shoulder is dislocated, well actually it's subluxated. I have a few small lacerations on my head and right arm, but that's all. But, more importantly, did the Citadel send you?" Sirin asked. Hopefully, she'd get a clue who these people might be.

"They did not," said the smaller woman by the door, which helped Sirin confirm her as the one with the feathery voice. She had an aquiline nose and sharp eyes, putting Sirin in mind of a raptor. Her movements were remarkably fluid until she would suddenly jerk her head or eyes to look at something with intense focus.

Sirin blinked in confusion, there *were* no civilizations north of the Citadel as far as she knew. Were they traveling as well? She couldn't think why anyone else might be this far north. Not that she knew how far North she'd traveled yet.

"Berne here found yeh and came to get aid," the bird-like woman said, waving her hand to the man beside her as if it explained everything. Sirin frowned; the woman had the air of a person who didn't like to explain herself, but Sirin *needed* answers. She opened her mouth to ask more questions, but Arndis chose that moment to reset her shoulder with a hard press that had Sirin yelping. Her vision blacked out as the pain blocked out the rest of the room, her heart immediately racing. Blessedly, it didn't last long, the pain melting into a dull ache as Arndis put a strong arm behind her to help her sit up.

"We will assess your injuries and then decide what we are to do with you," said the small woman by the door.

Do with her? She was a grown woman; she didn't need anyone to *do* anything with her. Sirin fumed. Flicking her eyes back and forth between the two women was requiring *conscious* thought which only made her more frustrated.

Near the door, the man, Berne, moved as if he would speak, but the smaller woman silenced him with a sweep of her hand and commanding look. Brow furrowed, he cocked his head to the side and crossed his arms, clearly annoyed.[5]

It was fascinating to see such a big man silenced so immediately by the slight woman. He was at least a foot taller than her, likely a head taller than Sirin herself, but the woman was clearly in charge, even if he didn't seem to like it. At Sirin's side, Arndis was splinting her arm.

The tiny bird woman crossed to squat next to Sirin, squinting at her in a way that made her feel like she was being measured.

"Why are yeh here?" she asked Sirin, sharpness clipping her lilting accent.

Sirin narrowed her eyes. They were *definitely* not from the Citadel, and the way they were treating her was reprehensible.

"I appreciate the aid," she bit out, "but I don't know it is any of your business. Who are you to demand my purpose? I'm a scientist, and my purpose is purely academic, and that is enough for you to know."

---

5. The people of Sanctuary, largely influenced by the shifters, tend to communicate non-verbally significantly more than other settlements of humans.

The unnamed woman looked pointedly at the man, stood and dusted her hands on her legs, and jerked her head, indicating he should follow. Before leaving, she turned back to Sirin, biting out "Yeh might want to wise up before we get back."

The man gave Sirin an apologetic smile and ducked through the low door of the cave to follow.

Odd, Sirin thought. *He acts so familiarly.* Surely would have remembered those kind blue eyes?

After they'd left, Arndis secured her splint and fished around in a pack the man had set on the floor; it appeared to be Sirin's own. She pulled Sirin's thick socks and boots out of the bag and crossed to put them back on Sirin's feet with a wry smile.

"An' I'm afraid Berne took your footwear," she said, refusing to meet Sirin's eyes. "He was worried yeh would try to leave and hurt yourself if yeh woke before we arrived. Yeh do strike me as just the stubborn sort who would try to go haring off on your own, even while injured." Arndis smiled, trying to put Sirin at ease.

"He guessed right. I don't like waiting," Sirin replied absently, as she was more interested in her pack. "Can you get me the jar out of the side pocket? I have some lunula in there. I'll heal significantly faster if I can get some in my system. You wouldn't need to worry about any of this," Sirin said, indicating her splinted arm.

Arndis moved as if reaching for her pack but then grimaced. "Ach , I am sorry. I don't—I don't, I mean..."[6]

"You don't... what?" Sirin frowned, Arndis was acting extremely odd, and she'd had about enough of whatever the hell they were playing at. "You don't want to give me *my own* belongings?"

Arndis sighed and opened and closed her mouth several times before speaking. "Well, once they come back, we'll know the plan moving forward."

"The *plan*?" Sirin sputtered, affronted. These people spoke as if she was a child, incapable of making her own choices. Or some sort of criminal. "The *plan* is for me to take some lunula, heal up, and continue on my mission. Look, I *am* grateful to you for coming to my aid, but I am here for a reason and I *really* should get going. You three have *no* say in what my next steps are. I don't have time for this! I have barely even started my journey, and every day brings us closer to winter."

Arndis dropped her shoulders, darting her eyes to the opening of the cave. "An' I think it might be safe to let yeh know, I think yeh may have lost several weeks' time. Berne has been tracking yeh for a week now and yeh were at least a week's walk out from the nearest outpost when he began."

---

6. I have also seen this "och" and can be translated most often as "Oh."

"Weeks?" That couldn't be possible. Sirin would remember *weeks* of travel. Wouldn't she? "It couldn't have been weeks. I swear I just left, I..."

She looked down at her clothes, which were definitely dirtier than she would expect if she had left only yesterday, and at her new boots which were extremely scuffed.

"But I just..." She blinked and gave her head a shake, wincing as it made her headache worse. "Oh, well...I suppose it could have been longer," she said after a deep breath, trying to understand. She could swear she'd only left last night, though as she thought of her clothes, and boots, and held her hand in front of her face, the cold unyielding truth revealed itself. Her hands shook with horror when she rubbed them against her pantaloons, hoping to rid them of their clamminess. Not only had she likely lost time, but she had no idea what had transpired in the meantime. These people, she might really not know them. It seemed that Arndis was trying to be kind to her, she knew, but the entire situation was unconscionable.

"In that case, all the more reason for me to take some lunula to heal. Once I do, any memories I have lost will come back. Could you at least hand me my notebook, maybe seeing my notes will help me remember?"

Arndis's lips pressed flat, she slowly shook her head and placed a hand gently over Sirin's pack.

The action shot fear into Sirin's veins, a slow creeping iciness that trickled through her, with each pulse of her heart. Blinking rapidly—Sirin realized that she truly had no idea who these people were. And that they might not have her best interests, or any of her interests at heart. "You aren't here to help me, are you?"

"We might be, it's not up to me to decide. As I said, we'll know when they return. For now, try to rest. I, for one, don't want yeh to hurt yourself any further. Please, try to relax. I am sure they will be back soon. Berne seems fond of yeh. He'll be trying to sway her to leniency."

"Leniency? I haven't done anything wrong," Sirin protested. These people were ridiculous, Sirin could feel her chest tightening as she recoiled.

"Ach, aye? Are yeh sure? Yeh can't remember the last several weeks, but you're so sure you've done nothing," Arndis sighed heavily as Sirin gaped. She held up her hand. "Hush, as I said, Berne'll argue on your behalf, and perhaps it will be a non–issue. I know it might seem like you've done nothing wrong, but we take certain things very seriously up here."

Sirin breathed deeply, trying to temper her anger. She strained to hear what was being said outdoors, but they were speaking rapid fire in their language again.. Tears prickled behind her eyes as she tried to remember exactly when she left the Citadel. In spite of what Arndis had told her, Sirin's brain insisted she'd only left yesterday. She *was* her mind. If she was losing weeks now, how badly was it damaged? She *needed* lunula. Who knew if the damage was reversible at this point? Hell, she couldn't even consult any of the memory-loss case studies she must have stored in her mind[7]. She squeezed her eyes shut, searching for some modicum of calm.

The conversation outside seemed to escalate until the soft-spoken woman cut Berne off with a bark. Moments later, they re-entered the small cave. The woman carried herself with purpose, crossing swiftly to sit near Sirin. Berne followed, face red and movements stiff. He crossed his arms and leaned against the wall.

"Well?" Sirin bit out.

"Well," the soft-spoken woman replied, "I am Gunna, a councilor of our village. We have certain laws, which you've broken. As such, you'll return with us to our village. Once I confer with the rest of our ruling body, who are currently reviewing the evidence against yeh, we will decide what to do with yeh. Berne has convinced me to at least speak with the others and listen to their opinions. Yeh don't seem to have malicious intent, but we cannot allow such breaches to occur."

---

7. I've heard this framed as a library or mind palace, but many Citadel-trained lunologists build an index for the vast amounts of information we can memorize.

"Evidence? What evidence? And malicious intent? Are you having a laugh? This must be a joke! You *know* my intent, I told you, I am a *scholar* on a research expedition. I assure you, whatever laws I may have broken, I never would have done so had I known of them." Across the room, Berne chuckled and shook his head. "Look, I really appreciate you all helping me, but I am on a very time-sensitive mission. I'll take some lunula and be on my way. If you would *tell me* what laws I have broken, I will gladly stop doing so. This is *absurd.* You want to put me on trial when you haven't even told me the offense? What are the charges?"

"Yeh trespassed," Gunna stated, as if it should be obvious.

"Pfft. Ha!" Sirin chortled. "Alright, look ma'am. I am sorry I wandered into your *unmarked* territory, but my mission is more important than some arbitrary lines on a map. It is important to the entire continent, perhaps the world. Here, when I can get to a bank, I assure you I can pay whatever fees or fines you may levy."

"I am sorry, that isn't a possibility. Berne, if yeh would," she waved the man over and walked out of the cavern. Arndis released a sigh, quickly packed her instruments, and softly apologized before leaving as well.

When Berne crossed to her, Sirin was overwhelmed by the scent she'd smelled earlier. Somehow he smelled of man and bear all at once, perhaps his furs were bear? He slung a wide loop of cloth over his shoulder before kneeling next to her.

"I tried," he rumbled with a lift of his shoulder. His voice was deep, and it seemed to resonate in her chest. "I'm going to need to carry yeh, so this sling'll help."

"Carry me? You can't be serious. I am perfectly capable of walking. No one has carried me in at least—"

"Eight hours," he interrupted. "I carried yeh here. With your head as it is, and your arms in no state to catch yeh should yeh fall, I'll be carrying yeh again. Now, I tried to get yeh out of trouble, but it doesn't seem like I'm very good at convincing. Yeh try and play nice, alright, and we will see if we can't get yeh out of this somehow. Though, I haven't rightly got any idea how," he said the second bit under his breath, as if to himself. "Ach, up yeh come," he said before reaching under her armpits and knees. She gasped as pain shot through her shoulder and arm.

Berne's eyes widened and he grumbled an apology as he threaded her legs through the sling and spread the wide fabric up her back and down to her knees. He carefully tucked it under her armpits, nestled her under one of his burly arms, and pressed her against his chest.

"There now," he said with a small smile. "You're a bit bigger than my nieces, but the principle holds just the same."

Sirin flushed. The man put off an intense amount of heat, and she was becoming quite familiar with his large pectorals. He tucked her blanket in around her and smiled sheepishly. "Don't want yeh getting cold. I know it's colder here than you're used to."

Touched by the small gesture, she felt herself flush, even as she nearly vomited when he picked her up.

They ducked out through the opening of the cave, Berne shifting a door back in place it looked like it could be early in the morning, as it nearly always did.[8] Even the low light hurt Sirin's eyes. She didn't have her goggles on, and after the dark, it was blinding. She buried her face in his chest instinctively, trying to block out the light.

He lifted one callused hand to the back of her head and petted her hair. "I'm sorry yeh feel unwell. I'll see what I can manage when we get home. It should only be a few hours, but if yeh need to rest, feel free. Won't bother me none." He brought his other hand to shield her eyes from the sun so

---

8. Lucky guess on my part, it was early morning.

she could look at him. He had a wide, strong face, with tousled hair and a beard. The whiteness of his hair had made him seem older, initially, but this close she could see they were likely of a similar age. "I've been watching out for yeh for a week. I don't aim to stop now. Yeh'll not come to any harm with me."

Sirin searched his eyes, trying desperately to remember him. He acted like they were friends. Like they had been traveling together for a while. She felt terrible she couldn't remember him at all but she did feel close to him somehow like she trusted him. She squeezed his hand shielding her from the sun. "Thank you. It's nice to feel like I have someone on my side."

Chapter Six
Berne

IN WHICH OUR HERO SUFFERS
A TORTUROUS JOURNEY,
FIGHTS A BATTLE MOST
VALIANT, AND PREPARES A
STEW

I T WASN'T LONG BEFORE the swaying of his
walking had his woman—no, *Sirin*—asleep on
Berne's chest. He could use some sleep himself,
but he pushed on, trudging through the deep snow
toward home.

Berne had set off for home immediately after
dark and had roused Arndis an hour or so before
midnight. Together, they'd gone to find a council
representative, and he must have done *something*
to piss the Lady off because Gunna had been the
councilor on call. She'd *insisted* on being the one to

accompany him, pecking at him to leave the other councilors to their rest, and considering she was the head of the council, he couldn't find any way of arguing against it. The trip back to Sirin had taken almost twice as long since Arndis's lemming form couldn't travel nearly as fast as his bear or Gunna's raptor. He could have carried her, but he was more tired than he would have liked to admit to either of them. He hadn't had much time to hunt during the week he was tracking Sirin, so he'd been living off whatever he could fish or forage along the way.

Hours later, they were well beyond the tree line and the moon reflected off the layer of snow covering the vast fields surrounding Sanctuary's mountains. Autumn had arrived a bit early this year. Only a few weeks ago, the tundra had been covered in low-lying brush, mosses, and vibrant flowers. Now, he could see nothing but white and rock all around him. Perhaps the variety of terrain is why he enjoyed his wide-ranging assignment so much; endless fields of snow got old quickly.

He sighed and looked down at Sirin, a decidedly more interesting sight. He frequently strapped his nieces to his chest or back while he did chores, even now that they were three.[1] They also tended to fall

---

1. The majority of people in Sanctuary baby-wear and it is often extended slightly beyond weaning, which happens most often between ages three and four.

asleep when he carried them. This was almost the same—right?

Berne felt something cold on his chest and chuckled when he spotted the source; Sirin was drooling in her sleep. There was something so achingly vulnerable about it, so *intimate,* he couldn't help brushing her hair off her face, just so he could touch her soft skin. Her cheeks were red and chapped from the cold wind, and he wished he had some cream to soothe them. He'd have to make sure he got some for her soon. Those soft cheeks shouldn't look so red and angry and it cut him to the bone to see them so abused.

Just like when he carried his nieces, Sirin's head was tucked under his chin and he was surrounded by her scent. His nieces' warm, cuddly baby smells always made him feel calm and fiercely protective of them. With Sirin, her smell seemed to curl into his nose and settle deep in his body; she smelled of leather and herbs and something distinctly feminine. It still made him feel protective but in a *very* different way. A way that had him wanting to growl at anyone who would dare harm her, which was likely most of his village at this point. Her smell both warmed and excited him. He was *not* going to let them execute her. Someone who smelled so good and fresh could not possibly mean them harm.[2]

The scent of her was a minor distraction and if that had been all, he would have managed perfectly fine. The sounds and sensations of her in addition to her delicious scent were absolute torture and made each step a struggle.

Berne was familiar with how carrying someone like this alerted you to every wee sound they made. He loved hearing the tiny sighs and snuffling noises when he cared for his nieces. His heart nearly burst every time they rubbed their faces into his chest, or smacked their lips before settling back to sleep. And he adored it when he could settle them with a deep hum and pat on their bum if they had a nightmare.

When Sirin slept, his brain interpreted every sound she made as erotic and every slide of her body tantalized. She would sigh contentedly and he would immediately wonder how *he* could make her replicate that sound. She'd moan and stretch, likely from pain or a nightmare, and it made him want to coax those sounds from her in pleasure, stretched out across his bed. Smacking drew his attention to pert lips he could imagine smiling around his cock and a yawn made him think of what it would be

---

2. I insisted that this was not even remotely sound logic, but Berne is quite determined for it to stay.

like to have her nodding off because he'd left her exhausted in the most delicious way.

The sounds of Sirin, Berne decided, were the most alluring noises he'd ever heard, and he longed to make a collection of them. He smiled to himself, thinking of how he might draw out an array of gasps, moans, and whines to begin, then build up to amass curses and screams, before ideally ending with wails and pants. Best and most tortuous of all, was the soft press of her body against his. The cushion of her thighs straddled his hips, making him excruciatingly conscious of the heat of her cunt on his stomach. Logically, it was the same temperature as the rest of her, but he swore he could feel it pulsing heat into him. Nothing had ever felt so indecent or right, except perhaps the feeling of her breasts pressing into his chest. Yes, he would love to make a collection of sounds and sensations. The issue remained, of course, walking for hours with her unconscious was not the ideal time to begin collecting.

Even worse, he was struggling not to make his *own* noises and alert Arndis and Gunna to the strain he was experiencing. At one point, Sirin rubbed her nose repeatedly over his nipple and he'd needed to cover his choked sound of surprise with a cough. He kept looking over at the other women to ensure they hadn't noticed anything amiss. Berne tried to position himself at the front of their traveling group as much as possible, at least from behind they might not notice the flush he could feel rising up his neck and face or see how heavily he was breathing.[3]

His only consolation was the physical exertion made it damn near impossible for his cock to stay hard; though it was putting in a concerted effort to do so. Between purposefully clenching his leg muscles to steal blood, counting backward as often as possible, and mental self-flagellation, he thought he'd avoided notice. The cycle of arousal and admonishment, blood rushing to his cock and then away to his legs, was exhausting. It was a horrible battle against his mind and body the entire way, but he managed. He'd never walked for hours with a stiff cock and after enduring this torture, he never meant to again.

His guilt played a significant role in erection management as well because it was the worst type of guilt. Sirin was injured, and in a great deal of trouble, whether she understood or not. He'd assured her this would be exactly like carrying his nieces and instead, he was fantasizing about her in bed and actively managing his body's attempts at popping a raging cock stand. He hadn't the faintest idea if Sirin would be even a bit attracted to him,

---

3. I will forever be disappointed that I was asleep for this hilarious display of fortitude.

and in truth, she might hate him for his betrayal. Here she was asleep and trusting as a babe, and he was imagining stretching her out on his bed like a monster.[4]

Just like carrying my nieces, says I. Ha! Just like carrying the girls my arse!

No, carrying Sirin was not the same, and it was likely a big mistake.

Over the week he'd tracked her, Berne had grown to care for her, and the thought of something bad happening to her made him shudder. He *needed* to think of a plan. He needed a way to keep her safe, regardless of whatever the council may decide. Over the past week, she'd wormed her way into his heart and he felt responsible for protecting her, regardless of what that meant.

He thought and walked and walked and thought. He'd gained habits from his bear and his bear's way of problem-solving was a favorite. When Berne had an issue, he would walk and mentally worry at the problem, slowly and methodically, turning it over in his mind, allowing the cadence of his gait to both spur him on and calm his nerves. He could examine thoughts and ideas, and look at them from different angles without judging himself for how long it took, or for how many ideas

---

4. I have come to understand that while this term is employed derogatorily here, many of the non-human individuals of Sanctuary and the Empire identify with the term monster.

he needed to ponder. It might be time-consuming, but he'd found this method of wearing down a problem to be fairly successful.

Eventually, his pattern of slow, determined thinking allowed him to have a workable idea; one that made his cock twitch to life again, sure, but an idea that might actually solve her problem. Berne wished he could talk to Sirin about it, but he wasn't sure if they'd have time before she needed to go before the council. And anyhow, they would only need it if things went *really* wrong, and he didn't want her thinking that was a possibility. No, he would fill her in if he got the chance, but until then, he would do what he needed to keep her safe. He squeezed her gently and unwrapped her arm, content in the knowledge he could keep her safe, even if it might complicate matters between them considerably.

S EVERAL TORTUROUS HOURS LATER saw them arriving at the outskirts of Sanctuary. The entrance to their valley was near impossible to find, requiring knowledge of the location of a secret tunnel into an ice cave and then making one's way through the labyrinth it held. Once navigated, any entrant would be faced with the Boundary dome. It could keep those who meant harm out, he was told, and it all had to do with intention. He'd never meant the village or his Lady any ill will, so he had no means to personally test it. The dome also kept the village decidedly warmer than the outside. They had seasons, sure, but they were much milder inside than they were in their immediate surroundings. Under its protection now, it felt to Berne like the dog days of summer, the hazy heat making him want to strip off his shirt. He could see sweat begin to glisten on Sirin's brow and he increased his pace.

As they walked down the side of the bowl into the valley, he could see the village proper in the distance. The dome simulated a day/night cycle closer to the equator, and he loved coming home at different times of day to see the whole valley at once, but the early morning was a particularly magical time.[5] The sky was a wash of pink as it brightened from a dusky purple, and in the distance, lights flared to life inside the many homes. On the far side of Sanctuary, the river flowed from underneath the mountains, splitting

---

5. Dear reader, if you think to yourself, this is just the sort of thing that would bother Sirin irrationally, you are correct. I still have no idea how this is achieved, or any of the Boundary dome for that matter, and it is a constant source of annoyance.

into many winding canals creating the town's waterways. In areas not reached by the canals, footpaths and bridges crossed over the water connecting the small islands. At any moment, the lunula would cease glowing as it sensed the illumination of the sun, transforming the river and the canals from gleaming streams of light to ordinary-seeming water.

In the center of it all, the largest island held a green space surrounded by shops and governmental buildings. Trails of smoke from breakfast fires hung in the air the rounded thatched roofs atop houses dotting the many islands. The council strictly regulated building styles when any new construction took place, ensuring the town remained true to the Lady's vision.[6]

Berne wished Sirin were awake to see it; it would have been impossible for her to resist the magic of it. Surely there could not be anywhere else in the world as beautiful. His best friend, Torsten, had traveled extensively, and he claimed he'd seen nowhere as stunning. For a moment, Berne debated waking Sirin so she might enjoy this as her first view of his home, but she really needed the rest. Her body wasn't used to the strain of having to heal on its own and doing so must be extremely taxing. He'd be sure to bring her out at sunset, he decided.

As soon as they approached the town, Gunna dismissed Arndis with a wave and gave Berne a stern look. "Take 'er to your house and do not let 'er out of your sight. We'll send for 'er once the council is convened."

Berne nodded and turned down the pathway toward his small house. He skirted the edge of the village, spying curious eyes peeking at him from behind curtains. He frowned, folks should know to mind their own business. It was normal for anyone to be curious about outsiders, it didn't seem fair to have people peeping at her when she wasn't even conscious. When he finally passed the last house and into the forest, Berne felt a heaviness lift from his chest. He often felt crowded while in town, but this time it seemed more intense. Inside the boundary, the forest held both deciduous and coniferous trees, though this close to town it was mostly broad leaves. He left the path to take a shortcut home, cutting through the woods. He wanted to smell the forest floor as he disturbed it with his boots. The scent of decomposing leaves and sun-warmed earth were comforting, and as he neared his cabin, sweet pine joined from the trees around his house.

As he approached his home a few minutes later, Berne wondered how it would look to Sirin's eyes. He'd built the place himself a few years ago, modeling it after the houses of the rest of the village, with a few modifications. While he'd built it with a second floor, he'd never installed the flooring for the upstairs. For the time being, it allowed the sun to reach the main floor and he hadn't had the heart to complete it if it might never be occupied.

At the front of his home, a wide porch held his rocking chair and whittling supplies. Someday, he hoped he could have a pet to sit by his side. For now, it wouldn't be fair, being gone for weeks at a time as often as he was. The thatching needed attention, he could see a few bits of moss he needed to rake down, but otherwise, it was a handsome house. The whitewashing looked fresh, if a bit patchy, a side effect of having three-year-old laborers, which only made him love it more.

Berne climbed his steps and cracked open the door. He gently unwrapped Sirin and placed her on his bed. When he turned back to the room, he frowned. He hadn't anticipated being gone so long and he certainly hadn't planned on having company. He had no guest quarters, his plants were dying, and the place was a wreck. Dishes were piled high in the basin and he had several projects lying about in various states of completion. By the Lady's grace, he'd at least taken the trash out before he'd gone on patrol, though he was fairly certain most of his fruits and vegetables would be rotten at this point.

Suddenly he was self-conscious of the lack of walls in the space as he'd never seen a need, living on his own as he did. The fireplace dominated the back wall of the cabin, with his easy chair and rug in front of it. On the left side sat his large tub, positioned so he could enjoy the fire's warmth while he soaked. On the right, a back door led outside to the privy. Otherwise, it was sparsely furnished, his bed to the left wall, the kitchen and door to the cellar along the right, and his round table in the center.

Berne wasn't sure her lunula worked the same way as his, but if she healed up when she woke, she would likely be ravenous afterward. He shrugged off some layers, rolled up his shirtsleeves, and dug through his cabinets and root cellar to see what he had on hand. In the cellar, he found potatoes and carrots, an onion, and some salt beef; he could pull together a stew. He poked his head out his back door and was pleased to see the bright red of a few late-season tomatoes peeking between the leaves of his raised beds.

The fact things weren't dead out there meant Cat and the twins had been by, at least often enough to water. He snatched them up and returned inside to prep and check on Sirin. She'd rolled onto her side, curled into herself, and tucked her hands under her cheek. *Adorable.* This was a side of her he hadn't been able to observe during the time he tracked her, she'd always slept inside a tent. Seeing her like that, curled up and peaceful on *his* bed, was beyond sexy. What he felt seeing her was some sort of magical combination of relaxed and aroused, which he never would have thought possible. He smiled and decided to chop everything at the table, so he could keep an eye on Sirin while she slept.

Berne had always enjoyed the slow, methodical nature of chopping food. As he finished with each vegetable, he dumped them into his large cast iron pot and followed it with the salt beef, and spices. He added some water from his pump and lit the stove. It would take a while to cook, but he could always chop up some hard cheese if she woke hungry.

Stew set to simmer, he turned, hands on his hips, and looked at Sirin. She was still covered in her own blood, and the last day's worth of dirt crusted her skin. Surely she would want a bath. He filled his largest pot and set it on the stove to boil before carrying several buckets over to his large tub and filling it. He lit his fire, pulled the tub closer, and dusted off the privacy screen that usually sat in the corner ignored.

Almost the second he had it set, he heard a soft tap at the door followed by his sister's voice. Catrin opened the door without waiting for his answer and gasped when she entered the room.

"Berne, what is going on? Everyone won't shut up about yeh having captured a—" She lowered her voice as she studied Sirin with her wide blue eyes. Catrin had white hair, like nearly everyone born in Sanctuary, that cascaded in curls down her back. Cat was nearly a foot shorter than Berne, soft where he was solid, and quick where he was galumphing. She suited her snow hare form as perfectly as he did his bear.

Catrin clasped her hands over her mouth as she turned to the bed next to her. "Yeh really did it? And yeh brought 'er here? Isn't she dangerous?" she hissed quietly, moving away from the bed.

Berne chuckled at her concern. "Ach, thanks for keeping your voice down. My *guest* is injured and needs 'er rest. As far as being a spy, I imagine she'd have had to *know* about us for her intent to be spying. She's a scholar, a ballsy one, I'll say. Problem is, she *is* here to find the Source, close as I can figure. Caught 'er trail a bit over a week ago and hoped I could scare 'er away from finding us. Instead, I frightened 'er head–first into a tree well," he said as he grinned sheepishly.

"Sure and that's one way to catch a trespasser—" Catrin chuckled.

"She's not dangerous, just curious," he interrupted. "She has this silly way of narrating her day and she talks out loud to things in the forest when she gets bored. At night, she describes everything she saw aloud as she writes it in a wee journal."

He smiled, remembering how she would stick her tongue out while thinking or greet the trees by name when she woke. She'd been so happy at her "discovery" of that "new" species of rabbit, the one that they'd been breeding for meat for generations in Sanctuary.

And there was the problem, she'd seen too much now. This close to the source, everything had more magic than elsewhere. She hadn't seen any modified animals that he *knew* of for sure, but the council couldn't account for everything she might have seen. She had certainly documented a fair few footprints in the time that he had watched her. Even word of one "discovery" by her could draw more scholars here, like bees to honey, which was the last thing they needed.

Berne looked up to see his sister smiling knowingly at him.

"Ach, are yeh back from wool-gathering?" she said warmly. Catrin was used to his mind wandering mid-conversation, and he was grateful for it. Not many seemed to understand him the way she did. It was part of the reason he spent so much time on patrol. If he wasn't around people, he didn't need to feel odd for letting his thoughts take him where they willed. "So she has a silly little way of talking to herself, hmm?" His sister asked.

"Aye she does, it's adorable, she—" Berne narrowed his eyes at her. "Now Cat, don't get any ideas. The council could decide to execute 'er later today. I'm just trying to protect her. It's perfectly natural for me to have grown fond of 'er. I've been following her for a week. She's not here to cause trouble, and she shouldn't have to die just for her curiosity."

"I know, B, but I haven't seen yeh smile that way when talking about anyone in a long time, and, well, we both know she's not about to be allowed to leave. Let me be happy for yeh. It *is* perfectly normal for yeh to have grown fond of 'er. Maybe yeh should let yourself in on that because from where I'm standing, it looks more like fancy than fond." Catrin went on tiptoes and kissed him on the cheek before rubbing his head with her knuckles.

"Ach, aye, I'll try. Me mind's just all banjanxed with it all," he muttered.

"Let me know if yeh need anything for 'er. I imagine none of your clothes are going to fit 'er," she winked and opened the door. "The girls are dying to know what's going on, so if it all turns out, let me know. They want a look at the Outsider." She walked away, waving her hands in the air as if an Outsider was some sort of mythical, magical being.

Berne smiled as he shut the door, but when he turned back to his home, his throat tightened, and his muscles were tense. They really might decide to execute her later today if he didn't stop it. He *had* come up with his plan that just might work on the walk back, and he hoped Sirin wouldn't hate him if that's what it came to.

Chapter Seven

Sirin

IN WHICH OUR HEROINE
ACCLIMATES TO HER
SURROUNDINGS, IS NEARLY
CAUGHT IN THE BATH, AND
FORMULATES PLANS FOR HER
FUTURE

THE SOUND OF AN unfamiliar female voice woke Sirin. Eyes closed, she listened to the bear of a man, Berne, speak in their unfamiliar language in hushed tones.[1] She hoped they would slip up or that she might be able to make something out. After some rest, she could catch a word every so often as the language they spoke seemed to

---

1. It might seem like I'm being pithy here, but I really did think of him this way.

have similarities to two different languages Sirin knew.[2] She just couldn't understand enough words to follow their conversation. The conversation ended with the sound of a door shutting and she heard footsteps cross whatever room she was in.

Sirin wanted even a hint of what they planned for her, an opening for how she might convince them she meant them no harm and to continue on her expedition. She was annoyed that she'd never studied law[3]. She had no real idea how to defend herself in such a situation. Perhaps she could offer to be helpful to them in some way. Perhaps she could help them improve something about their village, or even set them up for trade relations with the surrounding civilizations. They had seemed very isolated, perhaps they didn't know how much of the world existed beyond their civilization.

She frowned. While her head and arm hurt, she wasn't freezing. Her mind was foggy and she felt confused. Healing naturally was codswallop. She could smell a bit of smoke, but not an amount that should raise an alarm. Nor was the heat coming from any particular direction. It was just *comfortable*. The warm air was perfumed with a

---

2. Namely Goedelic and Cisalpaen.

3. In light of recent events, I can now legally practice law in 14 Compact Nations.

savory scent that made her mouth water and her stomach grumble.

Gingerly cracking an eye, she saw Berne's large form sitting alone at a small table. He was frowning down at a mug while worrying a bit of jerky between his teeth. As if he sensed her staring, his head rose and his attention was on her. The corner of his mouth lifted in a shy smile.

Oof, that kind of smile could knock a girl off her feet.

"Ach, you're awake then, I see. How do yeh feel?" He asked, raising an eyebrow.

She hadn't had much time to really *look* at him before, but more than anything, he *smelled* comforting. Another human probably wouldn't notice, but since she hadn't had time to dull her senses back to normal, she could detect his unique blend of the outdoors and the forest, something wild and free that couldn't be distilled to any specific scents. She had never seen anyone like him before, nor any of these people.

Below his thick mop of disheveled curly hair, a few errant locks fell over eyes that seemed so welcoming, so *familiar*. Sirin didn't have anything close to a type, she had been attracted to too many people to narrow down her likes to one set of preferences, but if she had, this man would be *it*. He was gorgeous, to be sure, but more than that, he seemed so *fully* himself and nothing else, and that was the sexiest thing she had seen in a long time. Perhaps ever.

"Feel? Fairly terrible, but I do have some lunula in my pack that could help me. Could you get it for me? It's in a small pouch on the side. I'll need some water as well if you don't mind," Sirin said, her tone haughtier than she'd intended as she tried to cover the thoughts she'd been having about him.

Berne stared at her, motionless for a while before he grunted and stood. He crossed to a corner where he crouched to rummage through her pack. He fetched a tiny mug and brought it back with her pouch.

He was a broad man, in a way that spoke of significant strength lined with enough fat to keep him warm in such a chilly climate. His skin was pale, and she imagined it would flush beautifully if she teased him. She ran her eyes, unabashedly, down to his thick thighs and calves. She bit her lip, yes, this was a fellow who would be able to manhandle a solid girl like herself. She would not mind one bit, she decided.

Sirin returned her eyes to his face, scolding herself. She wasn't here to have sex or ogle her rescuer; she was here for a purpose. Or perhaps she was here, wherever here was, to get *out* of here and *back* to her purpose. He'd been kind though, as far as she could remember, and gentlemanly, and he was definitely easy on the eyes. She decided when she left, she'd take note of how to get back, in case a tumble sounded good to him too. Dear Lady, it had clearly been too long since she'd had sex. Luckily, he interrupted her mental calculations on exactly how long it had been, by starting to speak.

"I'm sorry Gunna was so strict with your lunula, she didn't want yeh healing up and running from justice or something. I would've given yeh some in sips while yeh slept, but I didn't know if it would work for yeh while unconscious or not." He smiled sheepishly and handed her the cup. "Sorry it's so wee, I only keep one mug for myself and then these wee ones for my nieces. I've never needed more here at home."

Sirin smiled and thanked him before dumping a measure of lunula into the water cup and draining it in one go. His speech explained many things. They weren't ignorant, Gunna was just actively hostile. *Lovely*.

The familiar rush of lunula washed through her and she immediately set it to healing her brain injury and then her break. Oddly enough, the puncture wounds on her arm seemed to have healed already. Interesting.

She sighed and closed her eyes as the relief of healing went over her body, and suddenly, memories of the last two weeks rushed back. Hiking through the mountains, the increasingly deep snow, the bright sun. Giddy, she remembered all of the interesting species of flora and fauna she'd documented.[4] She blinked, remembering her fall, and how the bear had herded her. For a moment, she felt somewhat sad at the loss of her bear. He'd been her constant companion for over a week, and she'd begun to think of him as a protector.

She gasped, as she was hit with the image of Berne, in a tavern, laughing with his head thrown back in a way that made her want to throw away her worries and join him in his joy. Heat flooding her body, she then remembered her dreams, *all* of which had starred the man sitting across from her.

"You're the man from the tavern! That's how I know you!"

"Aye, I saw yeh at the tavern in Pershing. Ran into yeh along the way, thought it'd be best if I didn't let yeh die."

"Ran into me? Oh, after I fell you mean? I appreciate it, truly. But…" she trailed off, flustered from embarrassment when she remembered exactly how much she'd thought of him, of what she'd *done* when she'd thought of him. At least it somewhat explained her extremely visceral and instantaneous attraction to him these past few

---

4. See Proliferations of Life in a Barren Land by Sigfinn Gunnkelsson.

hours, after all, she'd been masturbating to her memories of him for two weeks. She directed a bit of lunula to clear the blush from her face. There was no way he could have any idea, so she'd best just change the subject quickly.

"So trespassing, eh? Seems an odd charge for folks that didn't have any warnings posted about private property at all. What is the sentence usually, anyhow?" Surely it couldn't be terribly harsh, considering they hadn't bothered to mark their territory in even the smallest way, and she hadn't done any person or property harm.

Berne took a deep breath and cocked his head. "That's a difficult question, particularly at this point in time." He rubbed at his beard before continuing, immediately triggering intrusive thoughts about how she'd love to run her fingers through it. He continued, thankfully unaware. "A few years ago, it would have been death and I would be in a great deal of trouble for not having already given it to yeh swiftly. These days, though, talk has been leaning away from that, considering it now seems our L—leaders, our original ones, I mean, didn't intend that. It's a very serious matter, but perhaps not one we should go killing folk over. Problem is, then, if we aren't killing trespassers, what do we do with 'em? That's what they will be trying to figure out and what we should perhaps try to figure out for 'em. Find it always helps when yeh create a problem if yeh can come up with the solution too."

Sirin stared at him, propped on an elbow for an extended moment. Execution? For trespassing? That was ridiculous. You simply couldn't go around killing anyone who wandered onto your unmarked land, but Berne wasn't laughing. He looked extremely serious and upset by the situation. She'd never heard of a culture with such a strict isolationist policy. It wasn't tenable long term. She sucked in a breath.

"Alright, so, if thoughts have been changing, have there been any suggestions of alternatives? As I said, I am happy to arrange for fees to be paid, or I could do some sort of service for the community. I have a fair amount of skills. I could teach or I could arrange for trade relations between you and some of your closest neighbors. My research is extremely important, but I suppose it isn't particularly time-sensitive, so I could delay it a bit if needed."

Berne shook his head slowly, his brow furrowed in thought. "It's not an issue of fees or service, it's a matter of knowledge. We don't want anyone to know about us, to know we're here. There's more to it, but I'm afraid yeh already know too much. Honestly, your research complicates matters worse. Yeh didn't wander here. An' yeh weren't lost, yeh came here on purpose. Ach, yeh were looking for something and whether yeh knew that meant yeh would find us or not, the fact of the matter is, yeh did. And the looking is the real problem because it *was intentional* and considering yeh already blurted it out to Gunna, we are going to have some difficulty there. I don't know we'll be able to convince them yeh were lying, and yeh weren't here on purpose. Looking on purpose, I mean."

Sirin squinted her eyes. Looking was the problem? If looking was the issue, it was because there was something to hide. No one worries about people looking unless they have something they don't want to be found. What could be so important to keep a secret that you kill trespassers? Something terribly important, certainly.

"So, what can I do then?" she asked, a tremor in her voice. "If they're going to execute me to keep their secrets, why haven't they done so yet? Do they want something from me?"

"I think what they want is to find some way other than killing yeh, but they don't have any ideas on how to accomplish that yet. I'm sorely certain they are not going to allow yeh to go home, no matter what yeh want to do," he pursed his lips ad rubbed his hands on his legs in chagrin.

"What, like imprisonment? Forever? For walking up a mountain?" Sirin asked, incredulously, her voice rising in pitch from a sliver of fear she could feel creeping into her veins like ice.

"Not imprisonment, and not for 'walking up a mountain.' For putting your nose into business that's none of your concern. Whether yeh intended to or not, it's what yeh did. I'm wondering if instead, yeh might've accidentally relocated here. Permanent-like." He grimaced. "We do have newcomers now and again, but usually someone goes looking for 'em. They don't just wander on in."

"Look Berne, I don't care about you or your people or whatever you have going on up here. I will gladly give my word I will never tell anyone about you all. You are so out of the way I doubt anyone would care if you exist. Certainly, no one is going out of their way to come to bother you all, or at least they haven't in—" She gasped, realization hitting her like a boulder to the face. "You're the reason all expeditions were lost. The ones that came up here from the Citadel!"[5]

Berne pressed his lips together and paled further—if that was possible. He gave a curt nod. "Likely so. We haven't had groups in nearly—"

"A hundred years," Sirin finished for him. When Lord Lagrath had explained the missing people,

---

5. I have recently begun contacting the families of those who lost their ancestors in these missions. Some are only distant relations, but I hope I can bring some closure to long-standing family mysteries.

she'd known that they'd existed. They'd been numbers to her, indicating she wasn't the only one who wanted to know more. But now…

"Likely so, though there haven't been large groups from your people in almost a hundred years," he said..

Now, she found she could remember her travels north, she remembered the closeness she felt to those lost adventurers. Their shared purpose and spirits had kept her company, and the unknowable nature of their passing had kept her alert.

Knowing what had happened to them, that they'd been executed for their curiosity, left Sirin shaking. She felt cold, sick to her stomach.

"And now I might be too," she whispered.

"Not if I have my say," Berne said. "I've got an idea or two that might be of use. There's been a lot of talks recently about these policies, and yeh might just be the troublemaker to force 'em to take a stance for sure." He reached a hand toward her before pulling it back as he flushed.

"I didn't come up here to cause you or your people any trouble, I only want to be left alone to do my research," Sirin insisted. "I came up here to find the source of lunula. It is an extremely fragile resource we know next to nothing—"

"It is, aye," he interrupted quietly. "And did yeh ever think the fact yeh know next to nothing might be by design? That if yeh were meant to know, yeh might have been told? Or if it was something yeh were meant to know, then it might not be so hard to find?" He dropped his head. "Ach so, I don't know if we can convince them, the council I mean, to let yeh leave. We can try, mind, but I don't think it is likely. Instead, I think yeh should try for a reasonable compromise, so it is."

"And you are trying to tell me a reasonable compromise is moving here? Forever?"

"Ach, what I am trying to say is if you're so intent on finding something out, it might be in your best interest to stay where yeh can look," he raised his brows and crossed his hands over his chest.

Stay where she could look. A permanent base *had* been a potential outcome of her journey. Ideally, she would prefer to return home with her research and bring the Lord Lunologist to his knees. If they let her stay, she doubted that meant they would let her leave to release her research. She chewed her lip. How much of her drive for answers relied on the ability to share them? Would it be diminished if she was bound to secrecy? She sat with it for a moment. She chewed her lip. How much of her drive for answers relied on her ability to share them? If she was bound to secrecy, then her research had no point.

Disappointment made her chest tight, and her eyes prickled with tears. She still wanted answers, but she either gave in to these people's demands or died. Yet, if she stayed, she could finally figure out everything she'd wondered for so long. It galled, knowing her research might need to be secret, but it didn't quell her desire for answers. And, she knew devious bits of her would never stop pushing regardless. She might even be able to find folks around the area to help with her research.

"You think that is a possibility…I could continue my work, as long as I stayed? I imagine I wouldn't be *allowed* to leave in such a case. Maybe ever." Her voice was nothing but a whisper.

"Might be. I imagine if they let yeh stay, it would be fairly hard to stop yeh from doing your studies. From what I saw, yeh research like yeh breathe. You're constantly taking those wee plant clippings and writing in your book. You'd be welcome, if yeh needed, to stay here, with me. Until, well, yeh get things sorted." He dipped his head, blushing.

"Well yes, I might—" She stopped. Plant clippings and writing in her book? When had he seen *that?* What *else* had he seen? The blood drained from her face. He had mentioned remembering her from the tavern, and *he* hadn't said he'd run into her after she fell, she'd just assumed.

"How do you know I have been taking plant clippings and notes? How long have you been following me? I don't remember seeing you at all since the tavern." She truly had no memory of him on the trail, not even a hint of another human anywhere around her until she woke up in the cave. He must be an exceptional tracker, she'd not noticed him in the least. The idea of someone watching her for an extended period without her knowledge made her shudder, especially knowing how she'd passed the time. It didn't matter how nice he seemed, if he could evade her senses for any length of time, it was evident Berne could be extremely dangerous if he wanted.

"Don't look at me like I'm some pervert, watching yeh was literally my job. Been following yeh for about a week, and I didn't see yeh much at all, so don't worry, I don't go around spying on ladies while they pee or anything. I'd *hoped* yeh would find your way back downriver, or I could dissuade yeh from coming closer, but I swear, yeh just kept on a'coming like yeh were pulled to a lodestone. I *am* sorry, by the way, for scarin' yeh," he said looking chagrined.

"For scaring me? Do you mean following me? I mean, I guess if it was your job..." She trailed off, shaking her head to clear it. "Anyhow it's not your fault I fell, it was the bear that—" She started. *Surely* he would have noticed the bear if he'd followed her for any length. Maybe he'd scared the bear which caused it to herd her like that. She *could* have missed his scents and sounds and dismissed them as part of the bear's if they had both been tracking her, but they would have needed to be extremely close. Or, she realized with a start, he could have been *with* the bear, making him feel responsible for her fall, after a fashion. As she thought of it, she remembered she could *scarcely make* out the bear's scent here in the cabin, it was mingled with Berne's scent as she'd noticed in the cave.

"The bear! Were you with him? Do you have some sort of giant trained pet bear?[6] Like for hunting? I kept smelling a bear nearby and I can sort of smell it here, too."

He chuckled and rubbed his chin. "I suppose I do at that." He shook his head as he laughed. "Aye, a giant *pet* bear. If it turns out you're staying, I'll introduce yeh."

Keeping a pet bear seemed extremely odd, but she wasn't familiar with his culture, perhaps it was entirely normal. Or, it could be part of his job. She could see how a bear companion or partner would be useful. Many contingents of guards kept dogs or horses, she supposed.

"He must be very well-trained. He didn't bother me at all," Sirin said, and for whatever reason, that made Berne burst out laughing. It was rich and sonorous, and it reminded her of roasted caramel. She *loved* the sound of his laugh, she decided.

---

6. I realize that I come off incredibly thick here, but the notion of shifting into an animal form was entirely foreign to me.

"I wish he was well trained or even had manners, for that matter. No, he's just a gentleman to the ladies and a bit shy, yeh could say," Berne said.

Sirin giggled at the thought of a bear being a gentleman, remembering her doodle of him wearing a suit.

"Well, I would love to meet him. If it turns out I am staying, as you say, that is..." She thought of what it would look like to stay in this place. How would her life change from what she'd planned? Would it be so terrible? She tugged on her braid as she tried to make it work in her head, only to realize her hair was stiff with dried blood. She recoiled in disgust. Across from her Berne chuckled and rose.

"Yeh might want a bath, if yeh don't mind me suggesting it," he said.

"Are you trying to tell me I smell?" she joked, mouth agape in feigned affront.

Berne chuckled, "Not as such, no, but if *my* hair made me make a face like that, I'd be wanting one, so I would."

"Well...I suppose you're probably right," she said, grimacing as she picked some dried blood flakes out of her braid. "A bath would be lovely, thank you."

"Oh thank the Lady, I wasn't about to dunk yeh in if yeh said no, but it would be a close one," he smiled cheekily and grabbed a large pot off the stove. He disappeared behind a screen next to the fire and Sirin heard the sound of water pouring into a tub.

"Yeh might need to stir it up a bit, to get the water evenly heated, but I've left yeh soap and a towel." Stepping from behind the screen, he gestured to a door on the other side of the fire and rubbed a hand behind his neck.

"Sure, an' I'm just going to...ah, I mean, I need to check the—" He flushed a deep pink and turned to leave. "Just yowl if yeh need me then? I'll be outside so I'll be able to hear yeh holler."

The door shut softly behind him and Sirin found herself alone in his cabin. It was cozy and she liked how the light scent of his bear suffused the place, comforting her with its familiarity. She stood, stretching her muscles and rolling her head. She was fully healed, but the rapid nature of healing with lunula always left a dull ache and a burn similar to sore muscles[7] . She shed her traveling clothes, piling them next to her bag, noticing that her sledge was parked just out the window as she stood. She gasped at the lack of snow as she peered out. The ground was covered in grasses and bright wildflowers, and Berne's house was surrounded by trees. How very odd. Perhaps there was geothermal activity in the area warming the

---

7. It's possible to alleviate this, of course, but it requires further lunula expenditure, which often feels like a waste.

soil? She couldn't wait to explore but that bath called like a siren's song.

From her pack, she retrieved her last remaining set of clean clothes. She hadn't had any use for them on her trip as they were not well-suited to travel. She'd only packed them in case she settled somewhere or ran into people. The rest of her everyday clothes were rolled tightly into a large bundle on her sledge. She hoped this set wouldn't be too heavy, she'd packed for the extreme north and it didn't seem too chilly here. She grabbed a pair of stockings, her stays, petticoat, and shirt along with the brown tweed skirt and matching vest. It was a simple outfit, versatile and functional. She was glad it was what she'd kept handy, knowing it would make her feel more put together and confident if forced to make difficult decisions for her future.

Becoming aware that she'd been lingering in a virtual stranger's house naked, she ducked behind the folding screen. A standalone copper tub steamed in front of a window that overlooked his garden and a pair of beehives. She stirred the water with her hand and sank down into the deep tub inhaling the steam in pleasure. The warm heat loosened her muscles and soothed her nerves. The gentle lapping of the water dampened some of her worries and allowed her to relax.

For the briefest moment, Sirin floated in peace, but the silence quickly caused her emotions to rush to the forefront of her mind. She'd always been one to rush in, to go headlong for a goal, consequences be damned. She'd paid for it repeatedly, but when she was the only one who suffered for it, she had never much cared. Her goal had always been finding the source, but her methods of inquiry had varied wildly over the years.

To some extent, her status as a lunologist had gotten her out of more scrapes than she'd like to admit. Here, that didn't seem to matter one bit, and it wasn't likely to help her. She'd been in tight spots before, but this felt different. She could likely escape, speed up her reactions, and bulk up her muscles and she'd be out of there in a trice. But after that, she wasn't sure. She didn't fancy the idea of wandering the tundra trying to avoid their guards. And that was if she could even find her way out of wherever they were. The urge to explore made her stomach bubble. Excitement or nerves, or both, danced inside her.

"Lady damn me for a fool," she growled, rubbing her hands down her face, "why did I think that this was a good idea? Will I never stop rushing in? Is this just who I am, single-minded to the point of recklessness?"

She'd thought she knew what to expect when she'd left. Death had been a possibility, of course, but execution had *never* been a consideration. She was facing capital punishment for what could be argued wasn't even a crime but an inconvenience. She could feel her panic coursing through her, but it warred with anger, vying to control the manifestations of her emotions. The quick pace of her heart. The sweat beading her brow. The tightness in her face. Each feeling heightened the others until they tumbled into a mass that threatened to whip her into a frenzy. She was *terrified* and for what? An arbitrary line on a map drawn by xenophobic isolationists? Her emotions bubbled up until she felt them threatening to spill out of her.

She sucked in a harried breath and steadied herself. As pressing as the agitation was, she knew it wasn't going to aid her in finding a solution at present. She needed practicality, and this disquiet would only get in the way of logic. The mindfulness training at the Citadel allowed her to work through her emotions more swiftly, and right then, she was grateful it had been a required course. She acknowledged that her fear had kept her alive and that it had allowed her to react to dangerous situations. But now she needed to use her wits to get out of this mess.

She dunked under the water imagining her fear dissipating into the bath, allowing the tension to pass away from her. She floated underwater

for as long as she could, using a bit of lunula
to give her extra time. Sensory deprivation had
always helped her think, and she certainly wasn't
about to dampen her actual senses with lunula
in a strange place, no matter how friendly Berne
seemed. Surfacing with a gasp, Sirin felt steady
enough to dig for the next emotion.

As she scrubbed with Berne's soap, Sirin was
only mildly surprised when she felt curiosity
mingled with gratitude. She hadn't felt any fear
from these people about her being an outsider,
so they weren't *actually* xenophobic exactly. There
had to be a reason why they were so insular, one
they wanted to keep from her. Sirin had never been
able to abide such secrets and she looked forward
to ferreting theirs out. Berne had even implied if
she stayed she might find what she was looking for,
which made her veins buzz with excitement. Ever
an optimist, Sirin considered the advantages: not
only was she close to her answers but she wouldn't
have to find some way to build a homestead in
a vast wasteland, she'd have civilization within
arm's reach. The last of her tension now gone,
she hummed with happy determination as she
worked shampoo through her hair. This was good.
Instead of living in a tent shivering at night, she
was luxuriating in a fire-warmed tub in a cozy
cabin.She could make this work to her advantage.

After rinsing out the shampoo, she found some conditioner and ran it through the ends of her hair as she worked to identify the next emotion. Determination. The council assumed her goal was to leave, so she'd use that as a bargaining chip. She agreed with Berne, the best course of action seemed to be to stay here, but she could easily make that seem like a concession during her coming interrogation. Meeting? Arraignment? Trial? It didn't matter, her goals were the same.

She swished the lengths of her hair through the water, loving how it flowed around her. She *would* find the source and study it. The council assumed she'd be arguing to leave, but she *wanted* to stay. That gave her room for negotiation, which she hoped might include accommodations of some sort. Perhaps she could even get the council to grant her research assistants! Sure, they would likely think of them as minders, spies to keep an eye on her, but if they could help with her research, she didn't really care if they reported her doings. If, on the other hand, they decided to make an example of her and execute her, she *would* fight back. She could be extremely quick using her lunula and maybe she could even get Berne to help her escape if it came to that.

The most likely outcome, however, was a demand for permanent residency. At least she'd have a place to stay if that was the case, but the blush she felt at the idea surprised her. No, it was a flush, not a blush. She was a grown, sexually liberated woman and she did not blush at the idea of staying with a kind, strong, growly, sexy man. Fate, or the Lady, seemed to be working to bring them together so why should she object? Perhaps she'd misjudged the reason. What if he hadn't been a temptation, but a signpost, pointing her toward the future? If she were allowed to stay, she'd be eager to explore *him*, as well.[8] He was unreasonably handsome and kind, and he had a way of looking at her that made her feel seen, truly, for the first time in years.

The lunula in her system allowed her to track her blood flow as it rushed lower. Her clit began to pulse as each wave made it swell with her lust. The force of it surprised her as much as it had back in town. She peered around the corner of the screen to ensure Berne hadn't somehow re-entered and then snaked her unbandaged hand down her body. She bucked against her fingers as she toyed with her clit, overcome with wanting. This was the strongest arousal she'd had in a long time, and she hadn't even used any lunula to augment it. Perhaps staying wouldn't be bad at all, in fact, the thought of having to leave made her chest tight. If that was what needed to happen to survive, she would

---

8. The title and genre of this book might suggest that I was successful.

of course, she wasn't silly, but she'd really *much* rather stay. Yes, staying would be lovely, in this cozy house with that big bear of a man. Research by day and some good natured experimentation at night. She could see it now, his large form hovering over her in the firelight, his cheeks pinking adorably. She hissed as she stroked downward over her hood, but the hissing sound continued after she stopped.

She whipped her head toward the sound to see a pot boiling over on the stove. She yelped and leaped from the tub, grabbing the towel Berne had thrown over the screen for her. She ran across the room and tried lowering the flame, but the controls were different from what she was used to. There didn't seem to be any place to control the fire, in fact there wasn't a fire box at all, just little knobs and a flame coming out from underneath a little grate. She growled in frustration and spun the little knob, shrieking when the flame instead jumped to another area of the cooker she hastily turned it back. A different knob made a noisy whooshing sound, but she hadn't any idea what it had *done.* Sirin returned it to its original position as she felt the door burst open with a gust of wind.

"Are yeh—" Berne said, as the door slammed against the wall behind him. "Oh! am I—is there a problem?" he asked, squeezing his eyes shut.

"I can't turn it off!" Sirin yelped.

The liquid on the stove bubbled over again and something viscous and savory sizzled down the side of the pot. Berne practically leapt from the door to reach it.[9] He turned what was apparently the *only* knob on the damn thing she hadn't tried and the flame shrank. Once he'd lowered it, he ran a hand through his hair and turned to look at her, slapped a hand over his eyes and turned back away.

"Ach, so are yeh hungry? I thought yeh might be, so I made some stew. I'm real sorry for barging in, I thought yeh were in trouble, so I just—I don't have any bread on hand, but I could check with my sister. She might have some she can spare. I'll just go check with her."

"Stew would be great, thanks," she interrupted before he left, "and don't worry about the bread. It isn't a problem. I wouldn't want to trouble her. Give me another moment to get dressed and that would be lovely," Sirin said as she ducked back behind the partition.

"Oh, I am sure it won't be a bother. She came by while yeh were sleeping to get a look a yeh, and my nieces are champing at the bit to see a 'real live

---

9. One fascinating aspect of Sanctuary is how much of their technology mirrors that of the Compact of Nations, despite their isolation. I've begun to suspect that the Lady might have imposed some guidelines on the world's culture as a whole because as it turns out, this type of cooker is fairly common in the compact I just didn't have exposure to them as I lived in a wagon.

outsider.' So, if yeh do fancy some bread, it won't be any trouble. No trouble at all. I'll just pop over an—" Berne said before Sirin cut him off with a laugh.

"Berne, I am sure you have seen a naked lady before, and I had a towel on! Don't make it a big todo." Sirin finished putting on her clothes and walked out from behind the screen to sit at the table. "And of course I would love to meet anyone who isn't trying to see me dead, a group which I would hope included said nieces."

Berne roared with laughter as he ladeled her food into a bowl. "Sure and they'd bother yeh even if yeh were dead, they wouldn't let yeh escape their questioning that easily, little menaces that they are!"

"Oh? They sound like my kind of girls! I love a lady who isn't willing to give up on a line of inquiry," she quipped.

"They are persistent, so they are. M'sister says they're just buzzing about yeh," he said, fetching a spoon from a drawer.

"Well, it feels nice to be wanted! Most people I know aren't happy to see me darken their door," she said with a wry chuckle.

"Are yeh pulling me leg?" He frowned as he handed her the bowl and turned to fill his own.

"Anyone disappointed to see yeh would have to be touched in the head. Why you're adorable an—" He cleared his throat handing her a large bowl full of a thick stew and refilled her water.

Sirin leaned in and scooped a spoonful. The stew, she was pleased to find, was hearty and flavorful, with tastes that comforted her palate rather than excited it. At the very end of each bite, after the savory tastes of meat and vegetables, she could taste the barest hint of lunula. As she lifted the water to her lips, she found there were traces of lunula there as well. At first, she assumed it must be her leftover lunula in the cup, but this too had the burst of the green, grassy flavor it only carried when it was newly harvested. As she sipped, she noted she was feeling the tiniest bit of charge from the magic seeped in from the water. Fascinating.

This close to the source, their water must be teeming with the magical algae. Sirin chuckled at herself, thinking about how she'd thought they might not notice any lunologists among them. Instead, they probably found them extremely young. It had never occurred to her that one might discover their talent earlier than at the typical testing ceremony. Imagine a five-year-old who could enhance their hearing, or turn it off when they didn't want to listen. Her mind whirred with the implications, at how instinctual their usage must be, as opposed to her own which was firmly founded in study and practice.

As she ate, Berne began acting oddly; he would look like he was about to say something and then close his mouth and shake his head[10] . He began speaking a few times and had gotten as far as "So I might have—" when she nearly dropped the bowl of soup in her lap at the sound of someone banging on the door.

---

10. Luckily I now know his tells and can make him spit it out.

Chapter Eight
Berne

IN WHICH BERNE PUTTERS
ABOUT, REVEALS HIS PLAN
BEFORE THE COUNCIL OF
SANCTUARY, AND FACES
THE CONSEQUENCES OF HIS
ACTIONS

A LOUD HAMMERING INTERRUPTED Berne's attempt at confession. He'd been working up to it the entire time they'd been speaking, but he kept getting distracted by how *nice* it was to simply talk to her. He liked when she talked and he didn't feel completely tongue-tied when speaking with her. Usually he was ill at ease when speaking with people he didn't know well and rarely felt the need to have whole conversations. With Sirin, however, talking hadn't seemed like a chore.

He'd much rather continue sitting here with her and see her settle into his house than answer the pounding. Berne was *extremely* annoyed at whoever was on the other side of his door and his nerves were raw. Trying to blot out the possibility that she'd be executed and steel himself, Berne wrenched the door open. Outside, Gunna, Jorund and Arnora, her fellow council members all peered into his house.

"We've come to retrieve the woman," Gunna informed him, her voice sharp.

"We'll be on our way in a minute, then. *Sirin* is eating now," he replied, trying to match the unyielding tone. The nerve of her, banging on his door like that, scaring Sirin so badly she nearly dropped her soup. He crossed his arms and did his best to loom. Behind Gunna, he could see Jorund and Arnora, refusing to meet his gaze. He frowned at them, they both opposed mandatory execution and while he hoped they would vote in Sirin's favor, he was disappointed they were letting Gunna lead. As head of the council, she conducted their meetings, broke ties, and handled some of the more mundane leadership tasks. But the council was an egalitarian body, and them allowing Gunna to lead this case had worry seizing his stomach.

"You'll not be accompanying us, Berne. We will send for yeh when, and if, you're needed," Gunna said with a look that had always made him feel small.[1] Whenever she'd leveled that glare at him, he'd always felt like a boy caught stealing raspberries from her garden. Pushing that aside, he took a deep breath and drew himself to his full height. Sirin couldn't afford for him to be cowed.

"I'll be needed right now then, I'm thinking. Because Sirin knows nothing of our ways, and I'll not have yeh tricking her. If I were to go before the council, I would be entitled to a sponsor, so I'll be hers."

Gunna screwed her face up and pointed a finger at his chest. "She's not a Shade, so she's not entitled to anything, Berne Brodersen. I will not have yeh choosing an outsider over your own." She looked over his shoulder at Sirin, who was standing now. "And you'll not ask him to choose. "

Sirin scoffed. "I have neither asked for nor expected any such thing. I maintain my innocence and that my intent is benign. I have nothing to fear." Sirin swept past him and patted him on the shoulder. "Don't fret for me, Berne. I appreciate the hospitality and your kindness." She smiled and followed the councilors out. As she walked past, Berne caught a tantalizing whiff of that scent that was distinctly her, but now mixed with the scent of his soap. She didn't seem to notice the difference

---

1. It should be noted that while Berne and Gunna share the same base accent, they still speak differently. Berne is much more informal, whereas Gunna's words come off more "posh."

in terrain or temperature, she walked out the door with her head high and back straight.

Berne grabbed his hat to follow, but Jorund placed a hand on his chest to stop him as the women walked away. Jorund was only slightly smaller than Berne, a retired ranger himself. He'd always been someone Berne had looked up to, but now he snarled at him in frustration.

"Berne. Coming right now will only hurt her case. Gunna will that argue your infatuation with the girl is swaying yeh. I'll make sure we call yeh in for your testimony later. She seems nice enough, Arndis had good things to say about her. If she isn't executed, should yeh concentrate on making the place ready for a guest? I see yeh only have the one chair; where did yeh imagine she would sit, then? Get the place ready for a lady and we will be calling yeh round soon as yeh know it," he clapped Berne on the shoulder before he turned and followed the others, who were already up the path quite a ways.

Berne watched Sirin's back until they disappeared around the bend. He hated not being able to follow, but he certainly didn't want to be a liability to her. So instead, he spent the next several hours tidying up the house to keep himself from going insane.

He tried to imagine what they could be discussing, but each time he made up a scenario, it ended with her being executed. But if Sirin was victorious, she'd need somewhere to stay as much as she'd need a friend. He could be both, so he wanted to make his house as comfortable and inviting as possible. Arranging a few blankets on the floor in a nest so he could sleep there as a bear if needed and he purred thinking about Sirin sleeping in his bed.

Once the house was spotless, Berne found several white rabbit furs and took them to his neighbor. The man crafted beautiful, sturdy furniture, and the furs got him a nice chair that he placed right next to his when he returned to the house. Even if things didn't work out, he told himself, the chair would be nice for his nieces when they visited. He yawned when he got it settled, remembering that he'd not slept in nearly a day and a half. Shaking the sleep from his head, he reminded himself that he needed to focus on his plan and get the house ready for her until he was summoned. It was strange to him, feeling anxious at being alone like this.

He'd always been a solitary person; it was partially being a bear shifter was such a good fit for him. But lately, he'd been so damn lonely. His house seemed to echo around him, the shell he'd built with a family in mind dwarfed him even more now that she was gone. Sirin had filled the space in a way that made his home feel cozy again. Her smell was fading from the room, and he already missed how good it had felt to cook for her. He'd loved sharing meal together, it was comfortable. He'd like that to continue. He'd like to come home after a day of patrol to have someone there. It wasn't that he needed someone to wait for him with dinner prepared. What he wanted was having someone waiting for him, to greet him with kind and loving words, warm arms to burrow into. And he liked the idea of that someone being Sirin. He imagined her, sitting by the fire, hunched over her wee books, drawing some plant or footprint she'd seen, her face lighting up as she heard him enter.

While waiting for word, he changed the linens on the bed, beat out his rugs, and even started a loaf of bread. Eventually, he found himself at loose ends and sat down with a yawn to review the laws forming the foundation of his backup plan. He wanted them memorized, so there could be no arguments. He had trouble though, his mind kept wandering to Sirin and what might be going on at the proceedings, or to what his life might be like if she stayed. The words on the page seemed to blur together as his lack of sleep caught up to him.

B Y THE TIME HE woke up, it was dark out. He cursed under his breath, and berated himself for falling asleep at such a time. He shot out of his chair. If they hadn't summoned him, they clearly had no intent to do so. Sirin had been gone for hours! Who knew what they were putting her through? He ripped his hat off of the hook and stuffed a few travel rations in his pocket, just in case Sirin was hungry. He ran the whole way to the town center. As he ran, he passed by people navigating the canals in rowboats, waving absently as he ran, his mind entirely focused on Sirin.

He'd never thought discussing the possibility of their death with someone would be so entertaining, but Sirin seemed determined this would work out, and truthfully, so had he. The possibility of being trapped here for the rest of her life didn't seem to phase Sirin nearly as much as he thought it might. He didn't mind the thought of her staying. More than that, he liked the idea of her staying with him in his house.

For the entire run, he worried, and he practiced what he would say to the council. Reviewing the words in his head, he chanted the laws that made up the backbone of the case he could present. If that didn't work, he'd have to *find* a way to get her out. His chest tightened when he thought of her leaving, of never seeing her again, so he focused his attention on the steady thump of his feet on the ground. It calmed him a bit, brought him back to his preferred stolid thought patterns.

It's going to be fine, he thought as he considered what he'd do to smuggle Sirin out of the city if it came to that. He'd escort her wherever she needed to go, see her settled safe and sound. Maybe they could even stay in touch.

He made a disgusted sound. He hoped it wouldn't come to that. It felt inadequate and wrong. Sure, he wanted her happy and alive, but he also wanted her to stay.

The large marble edifice of the municipal building loomed over the village, green in the dark. During the day, it looked damn cheery, but at night? At night it made him shudder. Was that intentional? The Lady did have a dark side sometimes.

Heavy wooden doors slammed open as he pushed his way into the council chambers. The room fell silent as Berne stood there searching for Sirin, and he growled when he saw her on the dais, wide-eyed and pale. At his noise, the councilors all turned from where they sat facing Sirin in a wide half-circle to look at him. Everyone looked exhausted, perhaps Sirin most of all. Each shuffle of his feet echoed through the vaulted ceilings, and several council members sat at their desks with a fork or cup halfway to their lips like he had interrupted their supper. Where the hell was

Sirin's food? They hadn't even bothered to feed her! The large windows normally flooded the room with light only served as portals for the night to assert its dominance. Berne looked at each council member's face, at each stern expression that fell in the dim light; so many faces he knew well were shuttered to him. When he looked to his mentor, Jorund pressed his lips together tightly and motioned with his hand, a ranger signal that meant danger ahead was unresolved. Great.

Sirin's shoulders were slumped, and she'd barely lifted the corner of her mouth to smile when he entered. He didn't wait to be told where to sit or stand. He stormed through the room and immediately mounted the dais to sit with Sirin. Berne rubbed her back, hoping that she could feel the calming message he tried to convey through his touch. She looked up at him smiling, and for a moment, he felt as if he'd done something extraordinary to earn such a prize. The smile trickled down him, warming him through and he leaned down, subconsciously drawn closer to her.

Gunna cleared her throat and called his attention back to the councilors. "It seems you've forgotten what little manners you've acquired in recent years, boy. Yeh were told that we would call for yeh if we needed you."

"Seems yeh *forgot* to call for me then, because yeh do need me," Berne said, raising his voice so they could all hear him. "But don't fret, I'm here now, yeh just let me know when it's time to say my piece." He settled back into his chair, doing his best to embody the way he felt on the inside—like a bear pacing its cage.

"The *researcher,*" Gunna said with disdain, "Sirin Agbuya has violated our laws and our sacred duty. The fact she did not know she was trespassing on our sacred land is immaterial. Our dictates are quite clear: No one is to know of our location, our task, or our duty outside of Sanctuary. As such, we have historically executed trespassers. Berne Brodersen, you've indicated yeh would like to speak on behalf of the accused. Go on then, speak."

Berne stood and looked down at Sirin. She gave him a stiff smile, and he took a deep breath to steel himself to speak.

"I've followed Sirin for over a week now. While she's been transparent about what she is searching for, she has shown great care for the environment. She has lovingly cataloged plants and animals and noted things about them I've never noticed, though I spend most of my time in nature. I understand our sacred duty, and I have ruthlessly eliminated others who threatened our protectorate. Sirin has shown the utmost care for both our land and our duty. Were it not for our sacred duty, I would request she be allowed to leave. However, I know that is not a possibility. Further, knowing what I know of her, I doubt she would do so." He chuckled to himself. "I don't know we'd even be able to run her off if we wanted. I think she should stay. She has a lot she can teach us, even about ourselves and our land. Beyond that, she could likely offer us perspectives on our duties and power we have overlooked."

The councilors' expressions hardened at his words.

Shit. He had a terrible feeling about this.

"I'm prepared to take responsibility for her," he continued before anyone could respond. "I'll ensure she doesn't leave or contact anyone and she won't put us or our duty in any danger. She could truly be an asset to us if we only let her."[2] He crossed his arms, attempting to find something more to convince them, but he wasn't a man of words, he was a man of silence. He could go days without saying a word. He hoped he'd said enough.

He sat down next to Sirin, who smiled up at him encouragingly. She placed a hand on his knee and said, "Thank you. Even if it doesn't work, I truly appreciate it. I feel like we know at least a *bit* about each other after the last week, perhaps you more than me, and I imagine that was difficult to—"

---

2. I am so grateful that all he said was written down, because I was too overwhelmed to properly catalogue his words in my mental library. I've made a copy that I keep with me to read anytime I miss him when we are separated because of work.

"We will recess to discuss our verdict. Please wait here," Gunna said, leading the councilors out into the next room.

"It wasn't as difficult as it will be if they try to kill yeh. I'll tell yeh that for free. But, look, maybe I've got a plan, just in case. Yeh don't deserve this, just for asking questions and such. I'll see yeh through this, somehow, I swear it." He patted her hand, which still rested on his knee. After a moment, she turned her hand to lace their fingers together. His stomach rioted at her touch like a swarm of bees had come to life inside him.

"I hope you don't mind," she said. "I could use a friend."

"Not at all. Say nothing of it." He didn't know what else to say; anything they tried to plan now would all be speculation. Thankfully, it seemed Sirin agreed, as she appeared content to trace patterns on the back of his hand, the gentle touches of her smooth hands were meant to soothe him, but they only stoked the desire for her that had been simmering all day.

Once again, Sirin was the most delicious kind of torture. She sat right next to him while being entirely unattainable. He glanced at his crotch, hoping his stiff cock wasn't too obvious. He wasn't sure what would be worse, if Sirin saw, or the council. Luckily, he was sitting in a way that at least partially concealed his arousal, but they couldn't wrap this meeting up quickly enough for his comfort.

Berne's nerves were stretched thin as fishing line as they waited. Sirin had pulled out her notebook and was scratching away. Peering over her shoulder, he could see how accurate her drawings were. She'd drawn a diagram of the village's layout as it would appear from above, leaving empty the areas where she had not ventured. It was spot on. She added wee numbers, which corresponded to the opposite page, where she made notes about different parts of the town.

She was acting so much less concerned about the situation than he felt, almost at ease. She even *smelled* at ease. Sadly, he'd become used to the smell of her fear, but she didn't even let off a whiff of it now. She tilted her head this way and that, scrutinizing her notebook, and Berne was content to watch her work. So often, Sirin had a vibrant, frenetic energy, like her lush body struggled to contain all of her; but now, she was so focused, every movement was graceful and precise. She stuck her tongue out as she worked, her brows drawn in concentration.

Berne leaned closer to read note number eight, next to a sketch of his cabin.

Design notably different from the rest of the village, set away. Indicates need for privacy and a unique designer. Likely self-built, as second story appears unfinished. Furniture indicates single occupant, though there is evidence of bear pet. Garden out window similar to those in village proper. Initial observations indicate largely temperate species of plants, potential for genetic drift, inv.

Berne let out a grunt; her observations were spot on. He cringed when he realized she'd noticed the unfinished second floor, but at least she'd said nothing about the roof. Sirin turned to look at him, her eyes wide. She was so *close,* he could see the flecks of gold in her eyes. She breathed in sharply and her mouth was open just a sliver, giving him a peek at her smooth little tongue. Instinctively, he felt the rumble in his chest start, the rhythmic purring of contentment he made when he was a bear. Berne clamped it off at her confused look; humans didn't make that noise. These days, he was never fully human, nor fully bear, despite how he might appear on the outside. Inside, he was always somewhere between the two.

In Sanctuary, it was expected for a person to keep the ability to make the vocalizations of both of their forms, so they tended to use vocalizations, postures, and words altogether.[3] Berne didn't see any way the council was letting her leave, so it wasn't like

---

3. Over the years, I've learned how to approximate many of these sounds even though its unlikely I will ever be able to shift.

he was hurting anything, but he didn't know how he could even explain it all. She jumped next to him and Berne looked about to see what might have startled her. He couldn't see anything but didn't need to wait long since she started speaking excitedly.

"Why is it dark? It's been daylight for most of my journey. Did we travel far while I was asleep? Am I just confused about the time of day?"

He chuckled at her excited confusion. "Ach, so—it's ah, night, just after supper time. I'd say it's dark for the same reason that it is warm. We are not farther south, we are farther north, but I can explain it more later?" He craned his neck toward the council chambers as the doors opened.

It all came down to this. Berne tried to steady his breaths. The council settled into their seats, and Gunna stayed standing, her back and neck stiff. From the back of the room, Jorund signaled that he didn't know the result with a shrug and a grimace on his broad face.

Shit. Berne's breath huffed in and out of him, and he clacked his teeth. This was *not* good. Gunna broke any ties in council votes and she did *not* like Sirin.

"After hearty debate and much deliberation," Gunna said in a clear voice, "the council has unfortunately come to a deadlock. As such, it is up to me, as head of the council, to decide the outcome."

A pause, and beside him, Sirin tensed. It was as if she, as he did, felt the chill in the room.

Gunna continued, "It is with great regret, therefore, I inform y—"

A growl was ripped from him before she could finish what she was about to say. He would not stand for this. Sirin was not going to be executed.

"Berne..." Sirin whispered next to him.

It took everything to keep his cool and stick with the plan instead of shifting and launching himself across the room.

"She's my mate," Berne sputtered. He was committed now and his blood rushed in his ears, drowning out the noise in the room.

"What?" Sirin and Gunna gasped at the same time. Murmurs erupted around the room as the councilors reacted. In the back, Jorund barked out a laugh and tipped his head toward Berne.

Berne took a deep breath and began his speech. He used his most official-sounding voice and made sure to enunciate clearly. "It is lawful for any Shade of Sanctuary, should they not find a mate within the Shades, to seek a mate elsewhere. The citizen must study any candidate to ensure their credibility, bind to them before returning, and vouch for their mate among the Shades. Outside mates shall not leave the grounds of Sanctuary alone for any purpose for a year and shall take all vows expected of any adult Shade." He took another gulp of air and continued, "During the week I followed Sirin, I reasonably established her credibility. I am fully prepared to vouch for her—"

"And you're leading me to believe you've bound her to yeh already?" Gunna asked, eyebrow raised.

"I have." Berne gulped, and looked over at Sirin with a pained expression and mouthed, "Sorry."

Sirin frowned at him, obviously confused. He reached down to her wrapped arm, the one with his bite. He poured all of the compassion and pleading into his eyes as he could. "Please understand," he whispered, "I'm just trying to help. Just try to trust me."

Sirin looked up trustingly at him with those deep brown eyes. Dear Lady, this might be the last time she looked at him like that. He'd asked her to have faith in him at a moment when he was about to prove to her he'd already betrayed that trust. He raised his voice so the entire council could hear. "Sirin, could yeh please unwrap your arm and show the council your mating bite?"

Chapter Nine
Sirin

IN WHICH THE SOURCE OF MAGIC IS REVEALED, SIRIN IS REPEATEDLY DUMBFOUNDED AND SUBSEQUENTLY EMBARKS ON A NEW, MORE PRESSING RESEARCH EXPEDITION

MATING. BITE.[1]

What in the fresh hells is a mating bite?

She was also fairly certain, considering everything she could sense from her body, her wound was completely healed. Sirin was not going to have any sort of mark to show at all. She shot

---

1. A number of societies on Caihalath recognise mating bites. I have posited that the people of Sanctuary incorporated it through cultural drift.

him a panicked look. This was his grand plan? This was his plot to save her? Couldn't he see there was no way this would work? Holding his gaze, she slowly unwrapped her healed arm. When she got down to the last wrap, she looked up at him to confirm that this was what she was *really* meant to be doing. She didn't relish seeing what would happen when his *genius* plan came crashing around their feet.

He placed his hand over the supposed bite mark and squeezed. Sirin's heart beat faster. Her pulse hummed through her veins. In that moment, she was completely aware of where he was touching her body, where his heat seemed to warm her arm and the air between them. Goosebumps covered her body and she felt her breasts tighten to almost painful attention. For the second time, she swayed toward him, overcome with reactions she didn't understand. She yearned for him to envelope her in his arms and *growl* at her.

What in the Lady's name was happening to her? Berne removed the bandage, and for a moment, she felt bereft of his touch. When she looked down, her arm was healed, but instead of smooth skin, there was a silvered pattern in the shape of a bite, though the pattern seemed too elongated and wrong for a human bite.

Gunna had crossed the room in the time it had taken Sirin to unwrap her arm and leaned in to inspect the bite. She pursed her lips and silently turned to return to her seat.

"And as my mate, Sirin has the right and the duty to guard our Lady's Secret. She is a citizen of Sanctuary by virtue of this bond, and needs only to be inducted as a Shade," he said with finality. As if that somehow settled the matter. "Now, it is late, and she's tired. I'd like to get her home to rest and privately discuss our duty and what she can expect in the coming days," he continued, sounding more like himself. He twined his fingers with hers and placed his other gently on her bite. Again, that *feeling* rose within her. She looked between Berne and her arm, feeling the blood rise to her face. Berne started when he followed her eyes, releasing her arm with the bite and blushing. He refused to meet her eyes and cleared his throat. This had to be the strangest sequence of events Sirin had ever experienced.

Amazingly, the councilors *began to pack up.* Across the expansive chambers, people stretched and shuffled papers into bags. As she watched, one man across the room seemed to darken, and wisps of blackness crept out of his sleeves. Another woman cracked her neck as *horns* sprouted from her head, parting her hair around them. Sirin gasped as people all over the room *transformed* in front of her eyes. She'd seen lunologists make some impressive modifications, but this was beyond anything she'd thought possible. She needed to talk to them, and ask how it was done.

What is going on here?

She was about to leave Berne to go investigate when Gunna stepped in her way.

"Berne Brodersen, yeh always were one to over-plan, weren't you?" Gunna admonished. "I suppose that solves that problem. By the way, I regret to inform you—" she paused, smiling wickedly, "—that your *mate is* confined to the village for the next few weeks while she undergoes lessons on our duty to our Lady. Following that, she isn't to leave the valley for three years. We weren't certain how to enforce keeping her here beyond that, nor if yeh would be willing to take responsibility for her long term, but I suppose that answers all that." Gunna nodded and patted his cheek before turning and walking away, muttering, "I've never seen a bear so hasty."

Sirin felt lost and bewildered as the council stood and filed out, nodding to her as they passed; a few even clapped Berne on the back and teased him. When they were alone, Berne looked down at her and smiled sadly.

"Guess the plan worked. I'll fill yeh in when we get home. For now, let's just try to be discreet." His face shuttered, and he led her from the council building by the hand.

On her walk to the council chambers, Sirin had been charmed by the thatched-roof houses, the canals and bridges connecting it all, and the tidy coziness of the settlement. She'd marveled at the warmth she felt, though she could see no source of it. In the distance, she'd noted a clear line where the snow began before the ring of mountains circling the valley. She'd been struck by how picturesque it all was, the main square surrounding a village green capped by the marble municipal building where they'd held her trial.

When they stepped outside, Sirin gasped, overwhelmed by the view of the village at night. The lunula flowing through the canals gave the entire village a transcendent glow. In the sky, streaks of the aurora borealis echoed the colors of the lunula, deepened with purples and blues, elevating it beyond charming to something otherworldly. She clasped Berne's hand tighter, struck silent for the first few minutes of their walk by the sheer magic of the sight.[2] She'd read of the lights and had seen them briefly at the Citadel, but never so clear, so vibrant or close.

As they walked, Sirin had the distinct feeling they were being watched. She turned her head to see Arndis peeking out from around the side

---

2. I am certain you must have seen evanotypes, and of course you can still visit, but I truly regret that no one else will be able to see it as it was then.

of a building, her face split by a huge grin.[3] She bounced up and down on her feet, waving wildly and clapping. Sirin couldn't help but wave back with an equally excited expression. Ardnis ducked behind with a wave as council members left the building, but the feeling of being watched only intensified as they walked back to Berne's cabin.

When she looked closely, she could see people peeking around window dressings to look at her. One person even *happened* to be putting their laundry out after dark so they could watch her out of the side of their eye. She stepped closer to Berne, hoping he could help hide her, she didn't particularly like the prickly feeling of being stared at. Luckily, he took the hint and placed his arm around her shoulders. Which, seeing she was still unsure how she felt about being essentially married to the man, didn't bother her nearly as much as she would have assumed. Her arm with the bite brushed his side, and she shivered, feeling flushed and exposed walking around other people. The night was cooling off quickly, and she tucked herself into his side, loving the warm waves of heat that came off of him and seemed to penetrate her center.

---

3. In my first few weeks, Arndis was one of my biggest advocates and has become a dear friend.

If people were going to stare at her, she mused she might as well stare back. As she did so, she began noticing things that were...—odd. It wasn't only the council members; it seemed people all over Sanctuary were different beyond anything she had ever seen. Sirin was sure she saw someone whose skin appeared purple, then she saw a man who seemed to have *scales* near his hairline that shimmered in the low light. Sirin looked up at Berne to ask about their extreme body modifications, but he only quirked an eyebrow and whispered, "Don't look so surprised. Yeh might've found more than yeh were looking for."

"Berne, that woman had a *tail,* and there was a man with scales on his face two bridges ago! One of those council members was emitting shadows or smoke or something! Yes, I would say that's more than I expected to find! This is lunology taken to a level I had never thought possible!"[4]

"Funny thing is," he said, lowering his voice, "they aren't even lunologists. Yours isn't the only continent, there's another continent, Caihalath and that's where all of the non-human peoples originate. We sit on the bridge between the two, so people from both continents live here. That man

---

4. I would say you can imagine my surprise, but at least at the time of publishing, most readers experienced a similar moment. I hope future generations can appreciate the awe of such a moment.

yeh saw, with scales... well, the scales are just the start of it. Truthfully," he continued with a massive grin, "the world is *so* much more magical than yeh even imagined."

Another continent? It seemed unfathomable. But, when Sirin thought about it, her people hadn't successfully circumnavigated Timonde yet. All the ships had either gotten turned around, ran afoul of storms, or had been lost entirely. There *could* be an entire continent out there they hadn't found yet, and it might even explain some of the weather anomalies they'd documented. More importantly, there were entire groups of people—*non-human people*—they didn't know about!

"And, these non-human people, are they all different? Like tails, shadows, or scales? Does it pass genetically, or is it random? Does it have to do with lunula too, or is it innate?"[5] Sirin felt a familiar excitement rise within her; the tingling suffused her skin, the specific rush of adrenaline triggered by a new discovery.

"Erm, well—I think it's not a lunula thing; they don't have it on Caihalath. They aren't *all* different. There are different species, though some can interbreed, which means I guess it passes genetically and—what else?" he asked.

---

5. Documented answers to these and many more questions can be found in More than DNA: The Search for Answers About Our Creation by Karoleena Rebexa.

"Fascinating! Do you think they would let me interview them? How many different peoples are there? Did they evolve separately to suit their environments? For that matter, what are their cultures like?"

"I don't know too much about the different cultures. Most folks here have lived in Sanctuary for long enough, several generations at least, we just have our own culture. Many are hybrids, too. My best friend, though, he's an orc, so I know some about their society, especially since my nieces are half-orc."

A giggle bubbled out of Sirin despite her efforts to restrain it. "Orcs are *real?*" she squealed with excitement. She could scarcely believe it! It was like suddenly all of the legends she'd heard growing up were manifesting themselves. Between giggles, she continued, "Next thing you are going to tell me that they really are the foot soldiers of an evil empire like in the tales."[6] She howled with laughter, but noticed after a moment that Berne was not laughing. In point of fact, he looked uncomfortable.

"They aren't actually the foot soldiers of an evil empire...right?" she asked, voice tight and suddenly sober with discomfort by the thought.

---

6. The accuracy of many of our myths and legends shocks me, which further supports my theory that the Lady must have imposed some sort of magical constraints, ensuring we don't stray too far from her vision for the world.

Berne pressed his lips together and shrugged, "Dead-on. They are trying to get free right now, but I'm afraid that's the history of it."[7]

It seemed not only the lovely legends might have more truth to them than she'd ever considered. "Oh, that sounds terrible. I take it they are not nearly as willing or bloodthirsty as the stories might suggest?"

Berne chuckled and shook his head, "They can be fierce, make no mistake, but no, they're not well-pleased about how the Pathian Empire has used them. I've never been down into the Empire, it's just too dangerous for a human, much like an orc traveling in the Compact would be. But I know Tor, of course, and the girls, so I can give yeh a few of the basics."

There was so much Sirin didn't know and she could feel the familiar itch starting in the back of her brain. An entire continent full of history and cultures that no one in the Compact had ever known? Her fingers wanted to fly to her notebook to document everything she could. First though, she'd need some solid data.

"Oh I'd love to speak with him! And your nieces of course!"

---

7. For a complete history of the peoples of Caihalath and their struggle against the Pathian Empire, please see Burying Our Oppressors by Megara Opalphine.

Berne chuckled. "Well, you'll have to wait a bit. Torsten only comes for a visit twice a year. We're working on building alliances with the rebel factions within the Empire and so he and his family are there right now on a diplomatic mission."

"That is disappointing," Sirin said, "but I can always document what you know, and what your nieces know. Though, aren't they young?"

"Oh aye, they're only three. They don't know too much, but I know they are eager to meet yeh. They'd probably be tickled to be interviewed!"

Sirin clasped his arm tighter. "Really? Oh, wonderful. They're your sister's girls, right? Surely their father could answer—"

"Sadly, he's out too. Raguk moved back home with the orcs permanently. He and Cat never quite worked out, and he missed his people. He didn't grow up here, just came as part of their first envoy and stayed for Cat. I think, eventually he just felt too out of place, so when they decided to call it quits, he went back home." He was silent for a moment while he chewed his lip. "But there is plenty of folks yeh can talk to! And Torsten, my friend, should be round in a few months—"

"Let's not worry about it now," she said, curling a hand around his arm. She wanted to dig in, but they had much more pressing matters at the moment. "We have so much more to discuss."

They were approaching his cabin, which seemed cozy now. He'd left some lights on inside so it shone like a beacon from a distance. The thatched roof and rough-hewn walls lent it an honesty that Sirin found charming. After years of living between her wagon and a massive stone edifice, this quaint cabin felt so welcoming.

As they mounted the small porch and opened the door, she asked, "So what about the lunula? I know you all are hiding something there; you have got to know about the source. You can tell me now, right? And why is your council so strict about trespassers that they were going to kill me, and what was all this talk about Shades and such?"

When they entered, Sirin's eye went to a new chair positioned near the fire, another at the table, and she spied the blanket she'd used earlier on the bed. She felt most comfortable on the bed, so she sat at the edge like before.

Berne blew out a huff and sat in his chair at the table. "Ach, so there's a lot to tell yeh, Sirin, and I'm having trouble figuring out where to start. 'Specially since yeh just asked me a fair few questions all at once." He raised his eyebrow again and smirked.

She was getting damn tired of that eyebrow.

That was a lie. She loved that cheeky eyebrow.

"Fine. One thing at a time, then. Why was the council even debating executing me? And what are they hiding that is so serious they need to kill people over it?" she asked. Berne held up two fingers at her, and his shoulders shook with laughter. Sirin had to suppress the urge to throw a pillow at him.

"Well, yeh wanted to find the source of lunula and why it enables a person to do magic. We safeguard that secret. It's the entire reason we exist, why we live up here. It's our duty to see that people from the outside don't find out about it, don't disturb it. Yeh see, we aren't even completely sure how it works or how it happened."

Excitement bubbled up inside Sirin. *Finally,* she would have answers. She was breathless at the idea of reaching the end of her quest.

"We can go see her, and I'll show yeh tomorrow if you'd like, but in the meantime, I am happy to answer questions and fill in what I can." he took a deep breath and waited, as if expecting her to ask more questions.

Instead, she decided it might be better to get a baseline and ask questions once she knew more. They guarded the secret fiercely. She'd begun to suspect, particularly during the council meeting, but hearing it stated so plainly was still a shock. She'd spent *years* working up to this trip. [8] Nearly the entire time she was at the Citadel growing up, she'd been single-mindedly focused on the source

---

8. Seven, to be precise.

of magic. She'd started prep in earnest once it became clear how little support she'd get from her peers. No one had ever seemed to have the answers she sought, but now she was getting them.

"Give me the basics, and I will ask about anything I don't understand," she prompted.

"Sure, sure. So..." He scratched his jaw and chuckled. "I s'pose I've never had to explain it before, and I'm not sure where to start," he rubbed his hands on his lap, and tipped his head to the ceiling.

"Ach, sure and first I'll say the Goddess—our Lady, was and is real. According to our texts, she created this world when she was young, based on another world she'd observed. She took things she liked and just willed 'em into being. For a time, we were like a toy, a dollhouse to her. She controlled most everything basically all the time. Back then, magic was rampant because she touched the world directly, influencing things how she liked 'em."

Sirin blinked at him. Logically, she could understand what he was saying, but it was a lot to take in. She'd never been *especially* religious. She'd say a prayer to the Lady when she was grateful or needed help. But Sirin had always pictured the goddess like some far-away Sky-Mother who didn't interact with their world in any meaningful way. She didn't think he had any reason to lie to her, but the very idea seemed preposterous.

"Eventually, she started to feel odd about us. She describes it as being both guilty and bored. She realized with so much of her influence, she was never surprised by anything that happened. We always did what she expected because she controlled it all. Our Lady, our *young* Lady at the time, decided she'd like to see how we progressed on our own." Berne sighed and shook his head.

"It was a disaster.[9] She built our world based on impressions of other worlds, primarily one, without any idea of how it *worked*. Sure, the basic rules of the universe still applied, but she didn't know anything about science or mathematics; she just *wanted it*, so it *happened*. When she stopped watching so closely, it seemed that the world started to fall apart." Berne reached behind him and grabbed a book, holding up a finger. He flipped through the book and nodded when he found a passage.

"She writes that she felt like she'd failed us both. We were entirely reliant on her, and if we were not entertaining her, then we had no point." He closed his finger in the book, holding his spot.

Sirin could imagine it. A fledgling Goddess, enamored with a life she saw elsewhere, would

---

9. Disaster is an understatement. Just how disastrous is only now beginning to become clear. I have reason to believe that the world needed to be restarted on at least three separate occasions, though other evidence points to an additional two times.

want her own. The notion of being a world full
of pets, or worse, ants in one of those glass
observation farms, was not a flattering one. Sirin
itched to snatch the book from his hands. Their
Goddess had written things down for them. Sirin
tried to suppress her wiggles of excitement that she
knew Berne would be sure to notice.

"So, she poked and prodded things. She'd make
a change, see if it worked, see if she could be
hands-off. She'd correct any issues and try again.
Eventually, she got us to the point where she
thought she could leave us alone, at least for a time.
Our texts—" he held up the book, "—say that there
was a hundred-year trial period. During that time,
she traveled the universe and learned about other
worlds. By the time she returned, we were almost
completely wiped out. The whole damn planet was
in shambles. The Lady writes that she made a
slew of changes based on what works on other
worlds. She went on, testing' and adapting; she
even brought in another god to help a time or two.

"Finally, she got the world to the point that she
felt we could last on our own for a fair bit. By then,
though, she was bone tired and wanted a break.
It'd taken her millennia to get the world just how
she liked it and she wanted a bit of a lie-down. So,
she decided she would take a rest. She gathered a
group of people, human and non-human alike, and
picked a spot that was remote and easily defensible.

She left some writings to guide us in our task and charged us with protecting her while she slept."

Sirin remembered hearing of at least one religion that worshiped a sleeping Goddess. She was flabbergasted at how ludicrous it sounded—and at how much sense it now made. The Lady was nearly universal among religions, an area of study for many of her colleagues. Scholars at the Citadel postulated that the recurrence of her among religions must point back to one original proto-religion that a group of them was attempting to reconstruct. If what Berne was saying was true, it made sense that she popped up in nearly every Pantheon or was the sole Goddess of Monotheistic religions.[10] The biggest change was in the sleeping part; most religions taught that she was actively involved in the world in some way.

"Which means, that under that mountain, just there"—he pointed out the window to the most imposing peak around the valley—"she sleeps, right now. And the entire point of the Shades and our village is to protect her and the secret of her location."

"Hence the 'we kill people who trespass' thing," Sirin said.

---

10. A colleague of mine has recently started researching the similarities between gods of various pantheons, in attempt to identify them and posit what their worlds might be like.

"Aye, though, as I said,"—he waved the book—"there isn't anything in here about actually killing folks, just bits on safeguarding and keeping folks away."[11]

"And, Shades?"

Berne rubbed the back of his neck. "Ach so—The Lady modeled this world on another, but it wasn't a copy. She pulled from their mythology too." He took a deep breath and seemed to consider for a moment.

"The man yeh saw, with the shadows coming out of his sleeves—he's an actual Shade. They are her guards and live under the mountain to watch the Lady while she sleeps. They can do all kinds of shadow magic things. Whereas the rest of us are Shades in name only, honorary if yeh will. We still guard her, but not as intimately as they do. I think there is a bit more to the name, but to be honest, I never much cared." He shrugged, dismissing it.

"So, let's say I'm buying into all of this; where does the lunula come in?" Sirin asked.

Berne chuckled. "Right, well, what she didn't know was how her physical presence would affect the world. Before she went to sleep, she rarely physically manifested in our world. We were like fish in a pond to her, and she was always separate.

---

11. Copies of The Words of Our Lady are becoming more widely available. I highly suggest it, especially as an insightful look into the motivations and character of our Goddess as she matured.

But now, she sleeps under the mountain, and her physical body affects things. She sleeps floating in an underground lake, and the sheer *power* of her presence warps reality. They say that time and space can change and bend in ways yeh would never expect when you're near. That's partly why only the Shades live down there and spend that much time with her. We aren't sure what it would do to the rest of us if we were there for longer than a day or two.

"Over time, the algae that grew there naturally fed off of the power she exuded by just being. They mutated, somehow and eventually, made it so some people, with the right predisposition, could change bits of themselves.[12] I'm not sure how it works, frankly, but you're quite familiar, I'm sure," he finished with a wink.

"The difference here is that we are always steeped in her power. The village is surrounded by a bubble, which mimics the seasons and day–night cycles from a temperate zone, so that we don't have to suffer the extreme weather and months of dark or light. It also keeps out folks who'd mean her

---

12. I've released several studies on the matter, and of course have spent time in study with both Dr. Calla Ghanim and the Dreamer Brier Ghanim, but there are always more questions than answers. Lunula have mitochondria, but also seem to have a second organelle,the called a dunamispiti, which that contains the power. These dunamispiti can pass through permeable cell barriers and seem to act with sentience, somehow, as if they are sentient.

harm. That's why it's night, but not as cold as it should be. Most importantly, that's why we can change more. So yeh can change, I would say, some things about yourself, we can well...—" he paused and took a deep breath, running his hands down his face.

Sirin was grateful for the pause because she'd so much to process. Most of what he said she'd dismissed as myth, religious ramblings passed down through blind belief. Instead, he was asking her to accept that those things were *real*. And not only real but more intricate than she'd ever imagined. She took a deep breath and prepared to delve deeper.

"More. You can change *more*. How so?" she asked.

"Well, erm..." He rubbed the back of his neck and blushed. "Ye remember my bear yeh kept smelling? Well, it's me." He didn't wait for her to react in any way; instead, he stood and stripped off his shirt and pants.

Sirin yelped as he dropped his pants, seeing him bare himself so casually made her blush more than she might have expected, though she was still processing what he said.

"What are you doing?" she squealed from behind her hands.

"Oh, fuck me—" he cursed. "I promise, it's—I'm just trying to show yeh my bear. Lady help me, I swear this isn't—I just don't have a lot of pants I can afford to ruin!"

His voice deepened as he spoke, and she peeked from behind her hands to watch as the dusting of curly white hairs on his back grew in length and thickness. His skin darkened but was then quickly covered in a pelt of thick white hair.

She'd seen people change their looks plenty of times at the Citadel; it was part and parcel of being a lunologist. This, however, was far more than she'd seen. He grew in height, and right before his head brushed the ceiling, Berne folded in half, his arms slamming to the floor of the cabin with a boom. His arms were covered in the same thick —fur, as the rest of him. She gasped when she noted a wiggle at the base of his spine. He'd grown a small *tail!*

Sirin was overcome with awe. Her mouth hung open and she felt wiggles throughout her entire body, urging her to investigate. What an extraordinary discovery! She giggled at the wiggle of that little tail and heard an answering chuff from Berne. She *knew* that sound, had heard him make it in the distance, and a rush of affection and familiarity consumed her.

Sirin smiled. Berne, looked over his pronounced shoulders at her, his now-massive bear face giving her a questioning look. For a moment, they stared at each other, silent and unmoving. The bear retained *so much* of Berne. She couldn't quite place it, but there was something in his eyes, his movement, that she recognized as distinctly Berne. This face echoed his as a man, and she marveled at how expressive it was.

After a short while, the large bear chuffed again and slowly crossed the room toward her. Sitting on the floor in front of the bed, he lowered his head and rested it gingerly on her lap. She'd been drawn to Berne as a man; how could she not? He was devastatingly handsome and charming in a sweet, quiet way. But Berne as a bear felt comfortable and safe.[13]

Sirin smiled and ventured to scratch his ears. The bear—no, Berne—closed his eyes and grumbled his happiness at the touch. She was surprised to find that the feel of his heavy head and smooth fur running through her fingers felt so familiar as if she'd done this countless times, though she knew she hadn't. His rumble soothed her excited nerves and the peace it brought her allowed her to absorb this massive revelation.

What she knew of lunula involved augmenting existing processes or slight genetic modification. Typically, lunologists finely tuned their bodies to

---

13. It's also just extremely useful to have a bear around that can lift or pull heavy things, and is as smart as a human for complex instructions. I cannot recommend having a shifter for a partner enough.

help them achieve things they couldn't do without lunula. Some lunologists finely tuned their bodies to execute their given professions to the highest ability. Sirin knew surgeons with exacting eyesight and precise movements, soldiers who could lift a horse and march for days on end without eating. She admittedly wasn't the deftest lunologist at modification that she knew, but changes on this scale? Her brain was practically vibrating with a surplus of ideas for applications now that she knew how much could be done.

She was so lost in her thoughts that she'd stopped petting Berne, and he wiggled his head in her lap and chuffed to let her know his displeasure. She giggled at this grumpy bear that was now apparently her husband.

Her husband.

They had addressed several things so far, but not *that.* Berne took his large blue–black tongue and licked her cheek. A deep, rhythmic, rumbling sound came from him as he nuzzled his head into hers. She giggled again, but then looked him in the eye.

"Can you come back? Or change back? I have a few more questions." She figured he ought to be able to understand her. None of her modifications had ever actively changed her thought processes unless that was the express intent.

Sure enough, he backed away and morphed back into a human. The process was fascinating to watch, she took note of the phases of changes as they overtook his body. His claws shrunk back into his paws as they elongated into hands. She could watch this process a hundred times and discover new details each time, she imagined. It was so *practiced* and smooth, but she knew the sheer amount of changes he managed internally were staggering.

When he was a man again, he cupped his manhood and turned away, blushing.

"I'm not used to someone looking quite so intent at me when I change. Hope I didn't startle yeh too bad," he said as he reached for his clothes. His back muscles flexed as he bent to put on his pants. His clothes had previously obscured how much muscle he hid in his solid form. He had a plump round ass that called to her to bite it. She beamed, surveying the expanse of his body that might soon be hers to explore. Clothed, she realized, he looked very much like a big cuddly bear. His nakedness revealed his more primal nature to her; she shivered in anticipation of unleashing it.

Chapter Ten
Berne

IN WHICH OUR HERO
EXPLAINS HOW MATING
WORKS, WORRIES HE IS A
ROGUE OF THE HIGHEST
ORDER, AND IS GENERALLY AN
OBLIVIOUS, WINSOME NITWIT

"WELL, HUSBAND," SIRIN BEGAN softly. Berne tensed, and she chuckled from behind him. He was not ready to face this, but they needed to.

Fuck, things were going so well. This, though—this can't be good. Time to face the consequences of my own stupid actions. Please, he thought, *please let her understand.*

"You'll come to know that before anything else, I am curious. I have what one of my professors called 'an insatiable need to know why and how.' You can imagine how I ended up here, looking for the source of magic," she said.

Berne frowned. That *was* something that had bothered him. "Ach, so it is. Entirely alone, for that matter. Where are your people?"

"I don't like others interfering with my research. My guild has been trying to dissuade me from my investigation for years. Finally, a few weeks ago, they gave me an ultimatum, either stop or be expelled entirely. So, I left. I had everything in place, and they'd made it clear that they wouldn't be advancing my cause. I will admit now that it probably wasn't my best idea ever, but these things rarely occur to me in the moment." She shrugged as if to say there wasn't any use fretting over it now; it was done. "Now, about this marriage or mating business. They truly believe we are mated because you bit me?"

"We are, but there's more to it. So, a mating bite is one of the ways that we are mated; it's often between those of us that are mammal shifters of some kind. Lately, we've begun to formalize things more often with a ceremony. I didn't mean to mate yeh when I bit yeh. It takes more than just a bite. And anyhow, I didn't bite yeh to bite yeh. I was pulling yeh out of the tree well." He paused with his shirt held in front of him. He tried to think how best to put it, but when he looked back at her, Sirin was staring at his chest. He felt heat rise in his face and cleared his throat.

He lowered his gaze back to his shirt, needing to *focus*. "It's a two-part process. The bite, and then a cleaning. When I was carrying yeh, I started to worry about what might happen to yeh. So, I cleaned your bite by licking—that's how it's done—figuring if we didn't need it, there was no harm done. Yeh would see a scar and just heal it. That way, though, we would have an option if they were truly intent on execution." He slumped into the chair at the table, arms on his large thighs, and hung his head. Would she even understand? It sounded so stupid when he said it out loud. It must sound like a crock of shit to her. He thought she might be masking her scent, or perhaps she was really as calm as she looked. He took a deep breath and attacked the crux of the matter.

"I am sorry I trapped yeh here with me. But, I just couldn't let yeh die after—after I got to know yeh. And, I know I didn't really *meet* meet yeh until this morning, but I've been following yeh for longer than a week and I just... felt like I knew yeh. Like yeh were already my friend. I never meant to trap yeh."

She was quiet for longer than he'd have liked, and he realized how much of his people's communication was non-verbal. With Sirin, she didn't make any of the subtle noises or movements he expected; her body language was so different as to be incomprehensible.

"You were *supposed* to kill me. That was your job.[1] But you didn't. Why?" Sirin asked, eyeing him.

Berne cleared his throat. He hadn't expected that question. "I asked myself the same thing. At first, yeh just interested me. And yeh weren't too close yet, so I thought I might just watch over yeh for a bit." He inhaled, pushing his chest out and rubbing near his clavicle at the ache that had started there. "Catrin and I had a younger sister, Annika. She died when she was fifteen. She was out, studying for her shifted form, so it's not uncommon for us to be gone for a bit." He closed his eyes and took a steadying breath before continuing. "She never came back. We looked for weeks. Eventually, we found some of her things with some—remains. I've always wished someone had been there for her. That I coulda done something. I think I just didn't want someone else to die for no reason."

Sirin nodded, a sad look crossing her face. Her scent spiked as she murmured, "I am so sorry you had to experience that. It's never easy to lose people you love."

---

1. Shortly after these events, the council of Sanctuary clarified their rulings around trespassing, which involved a sliding scale of infractions and corresponding responses. Until the Barrier fell, they worked swimmingly.

"No," he whispered. The pain had lessened with time, but it would never be gone.[2] "But that wasn't the only reason, I think. Yeh sparked my interest, I s'pose. Yeh were so vibrant. The more I watched yeh, the more it seemed a shame to lose that, like the world would be less for your absence. Eventually, I felt like I knew yeh, and by then it just wasn't an option, no matter what I tried to tell myself."

Sirin blushed and he sucked in a breath. She was beautiful, with her deep eyes and lush curves, but when she blushed, she seemed to *glow* with it.

"Thank you. For saving me," she said. She smiled, looking away from him. "And to be honest, I *am* grateful I get to stay and continue my research. I'm not sure how to navigate—this." She indicated between them.

"Well, I'm afraid you'll have to stay with me. If it doesn't seem like a true mating, they might go back on their word. So, at least yeh won't need to find a place to live. I'll not ask anything of yeh that isn't freely given. I'll not pressure yeh for favors at all, so yeh don't need to worry on that account. You're welcome to the bed. I can sleep as my bear on the floor and be perfectly comfortable. Yeh don't—" His words caught in his throat, sticky with guilt. "Yeh don't have someone I am keeping yeh from now?"

---

2. Though admittedly, answers about Annika did help ease his pain.

The worry echoed through his head. It was one thing if they needed to learn how to get along, to learn to love one another, but that would never be possible if he had taken her from someone she loved.

"Berne, you didn't steal me from anyone," she assured. "You think anyone I was in a relationship with would let me go haring off into the wilderness alone like this?"

He scoffed, "Sure, I'd not. I'll tell yeh that." It was dangerous for *anyone* to be out there alone, let alone someone as obviously delectable as Sirin. He'd chased off three separate predators while following her.

Sirin raised an eyebrow.[3] "Mmm, well—as I said, I am happy to be here, where I conduct my research. Truth be told, this was a scouting mission. If I found something that required extended study, I was prepared to stay wherever I needed long-term." She rubbed his shoulder and he nodded. She took a deep breath and continued. "And you? Am I now keeping you from someone? Have I not trapped you just as much?"

He snapped his head up to look at her. "No. There's no one. And yeh haven't trapped me at all.

---

3. Astute readers will likely deduce that while we've always been deeply in love, we've also had our fair share of power struggles, especially concerning what Berne likes to call my "harebrained schemes."

Yeh likely saved me a deal of trouble. There's no one here for me, so I was trying to decide if it was worth it to try to leave to find a mate. I'm not great with people as it is. This is the most I have spoken in months." He lifted a shoulder dejectedly.

"I was torn because I have always wanted bairns, but I just couldn't see how I was going to leave and integrate into society enough to meet someone. How I was going to determine if they'd fit, if I could trust them? You're—you're like a gift. Like I said, I'll not ask for anything, but you're more than I ever considered hoping for, and I would be lying if I said I didn't hope yeh could come to want me back in time."

She lifted a hand to brush hairs away from his face before cupping his cheek. "We *did* come to know each other out there, in a way. And I do think we have started a friendship. The way I see it, there are worse foundations for a marriage than friendship and desire."

Her words flashed through him, fizzing along his skin and settling in his groin. This was more than he ever hoped, more than—No, this wasn't fair to Sirin. She never asked for this. He *tricked* her and now she was stuck here. Sure, she meant to come here, but she hadn't signed up for a long-term relationship. He needed to make it very clear he wasn't looking for anything she didn't absolutely want. Because he *wanted* her with everything he had, but if she didn't want him, he wasn't interested. "Sirin, I told yeh, I wouldn't dare presume—"

"Oh shut up, you silly bear," she said with a blush. "Is it so hard to believe I might want you back, as you hoped? Or is it that you don't want *me?*"

He moved to speak, to tell her that was decidedly not the case, but she placed her hand back on his face, her thumb resting on his lips. Berne inhaled sharply as her thumb ghosted across his lips, his cock thickening instantly. That light touch ignited his veins, desire pulsing through him.

"Berne, I'm not some blushing, inexperienced miss. I'm not going to play coy with you." Sirin lowered her voice, her deep whisper dragging along his skin. "These breaths, your pulse, that hardness in your trousers, they tell me yeh *might* want me back. I know what *I* want, Berne, and now I have a husband. I find I want to... *explore* him. But I need yeh to tell me what *yeh* want."

He'd steeled himself, prepared for the inevitability she wouldn't want him, that she wouldn't reciprocate the soul-crushing *need* he felt for her. Resigned himself to fast releases in the woods behind his house until she welcomed him into what he now thought of as her bed.

He should've known when he'd run into her in the forest. Her scent on the breeze, her excited gasp, and her gleeful dance had made him smile stupidly, his large tongue hanging out of his mouth. He marveled at how only yesterday he'd thought he was still torn about what to do with her when he'd already been careening toward her. He should have known she would have his heart, and his cock, in her hands for the taking.

Berne's breath punched out of him at her words, and he swallowed before speaking. With his luck, his voice would crack like a cub's if he didn't.

"I'm here, for your exploring if you'd like." Sitting with his arms wide, he indicated he was hers to command. He hoped she didn't look too closely at his hands, which trembled like the last stubborn leaves of autumn. Berne wasn't exactly inexperienced either, but it had been quite some time, and he didn't think he'd ever wanted anyone near as much. Did he even properly remember what to *do?* He would come the second she touched him if he wasn't careful.

She pursed her lips for a moment, immediately causing him to imagine them wrapped around his shaft, and he groaned despite himself. He could imagine how fucking delicious she would look, how slick, how hot she'd feel wrapped around him. How he was in *so much fucking trouble.*

Goddess damn yeh for an idiot, Berne. Could yeh not have taken five fucking minutes before falling asleep to wank off so yeh don't go off like a volcano.

Sirin braced herself on his leg, stood with the smallest smirk, and moved to stand between his legs. Which put her round, little breasts at his eye level, torturing him with their closeness. She smiled deviously, Sirin knew exactly what she was doing to him, as she sat her lush bottom on his knee.

Seated on his lap, her hips and wonderfully thick thighs—*so close* to his cock which was already stone hard—were temptation personified. The image of himself rutting between them raged through him. She raised her arms, winding her hands into the hair at the nape of his neck, making him growl.

He was going to blow in his pants like a schoolboy if he wasn't careful.

Sirin looked him in the eye, her lips an inch away from his own. The smallest movement would have them kissing.

"All *mine to explore?* Wherever shall I start?" She bit her luscious lip and seemed to consider, leaning into his neck to whisper, "The neck is always a good place but"—she tilted her head and grazed his ear with her lips—"I *am* always interested in an ear nibble." She took his earlobe in her mouth and gave it the slightest nip.

His heart beat faster, and he closed his eyes with a sigh, allowing himself to just *feel* her.

"Though, I have to admit," she whispered, grabbing his chin to turn his face to hers, "a kiss can tell you so much about what to expect from a lover."

Sirin's mouth hovered over his, their breath mingling between them. She licked her lips, their eyes meeting, before gently brushing her lips over his. The touch was like a spark, kindling his desire and spurring him to action. He *needed* to touch her everywhere. He wrapped his arms around her, squeezing the outside of her thigh.

Berne caught her lips with his and wasted no time with small, sipping kisses. He would, he marveled, have *years* of leisurely caressing kisses. Right now, he *needed* to plunder her mouth with deep stroking slides of tongue and teeth, to suck her plump lower lip and drink down her moans. Her taste reminded him of everything he loved about the forest, wild brightness dancing along his tongue tempered by a deep, smooth richness that grounded him in the present.

She kissed fiercely as if her very life depended on it, and in a way, he supposed, it had. When he broke his mouth from hers, she let out a sound of disappointment, chasing his lips before he ducked to graze his mouth over her neck and shoulder. The sigh she released, full of yearning and desire, as he fastened his lips to her skin was more than he could've hoped for during his uncomfortable walk. She clung to his hair, guiding him where she wanted him most. He licked the shell of her ear, chuckling at her gasp when he sucked her earlobe into his mouth. He laved her with his lips and tongue, reminding them of how he'd like to treat her pussy. She writhed in his lap, her hands blindly scrabbling at his clothes, searching for skin. She'd already thrown her vest to the floor next to them, and had, at some point, unbuttoned half of her blouse.

Berne raised a hand to grasp her forearm, seeking their mating bite. He *needed* to touch her there. It bound her to him, made him lucky enough to have such a juicy morsel wiggling on his thighs. While he'd never had an interest in an arm before, it had suddenly become ridiculously alluring. He transferred his mouth to her arm, and when he sucked on the spot until Sirin's eyes went glassy. She threw her head back, pants falling heavily from her parted lips. He'd heard mate bites were extremely sensitive, but this was beyond what he'd expected. Her scent had taken on the deeper, muskier scent of her arousal and he gulped it down; he was parched, and she was the only thing that could quench his thirst. Sirin rubbed her legs together and gave a needy whimper.

"I need—I need you. Take me to bed, *now*," she ordered in a tortured whisper.

Berne swept her up and deposited her onto their bed. He smiled to himself, already thinking of it as *theirs* when moments ago, he'd thought of it as *hers* alone. There was something so intensely gratifying about *their* bed. Thinking about the smell of her sex mingling with his own on the sheets made him bite his lip as he palmed his cock through his pants.

For a moment, he allowed himself to just *look* at her. For over a week, he hadn't had any real idea of what her body was like under her thick layers, but he couldn't imagine being more pleased with what she revealed to him. Her skirts had slipped up her legs, exposing voluptuous thighs encased in thick woolen stockings. Her long, deep umber hair had, at some point, fallen from her bun. It spread across the bed behind her, like ink he could already feel seeping in, coloring and flooding the cracks in his life. Her mouth glistened the most alluring shade of dusky pink-brown, one he hoped matched the tips of the perfect little breasts heaving under her bodice. He wanted to unwrap her like a present, pull the ties that bound her and remove the fabrics that hid her glorious body from him. But, apparently, that would take too long.

Sirin raised her legs to remove her boots and chuck them to the floor. Berne smiled wickedly because, in her haste, she'd revealed the most perfect thatch of dark curls and glistening mahogany sex to him. His mouth watered for her, ready to drink in the slickness that dewed at the edges.

A frustrated scoff tore him from his fantasy. "Well? You're wearing too many clothes!" she admonished while frantically unbuttoning her blouse so it hung open over her stays.

"Yeh *are* an impatient one, aren't yeh?" He chuckled as he raised his shirt over his head, tossing it down. He reached down to help her ease out of her own, pausing to kiss the indignant look off of her face. She giggled into their kiss, and Berne couldn't resist tickling as he untied her side lacing stays. He ran his hands up the sides of her ribs, skating over her skin and drawing peals of laughter with his fingers. He watched the ripples of her body as she squirmed under his touch, revealing her expanses of soft, delectable skin. The heat of his desire was fierce and demanding, but this other fervor felt steady and firm—enduring.

With her clothes clutched in his hand, he let out a pleased grumble and ran his tongue over her pert breast. He nuzzled the valley between them before latching on to her erect nipple, sucking and rolling it around his mouth. After several strong pulls had her arching off the bed, he moved to give the other the same treatment, abandoning her clothes in favor of caressing her side and untying her skirts. He nipped her breast goodbye, already anticipating his return, kissing his way down the soft round of her belly. Then, with the most delicious slowness, he eased her skirts down to the floor, allowing him to bury his nose between her thighs and drink in her scent. He inhaled, luxuriating in being surrounded by her complex perfume, her sounds all he could hear. His entire world narrowed and centered on her. Sirin made him *hungry* in the most carnal way, and he thought he might have growled in desperate approval.

Berne placed small, reverent kisses and licks along the crease of her thighs, pausing every so often to nuzzle in and enjoy the scent of her. He ran his hands up the insides of her strong legs, pressing his thumbs to her mound to spread her wide for his view. Berne glanced at her face; Sirin's cheeks and chest were flushed, her mouth open on a pant as she stared down at him, desperation in her dark gaze.

He was pleased to see how needy she was, how lost to him, but grumbled when he realized she was awkwardly lifting her head to watch him. That would never do. He quickly grabbed his pillow, tucking it under her head, with a peck to her kiss-swollen lips, devouring her giggle. He ran his hands down her arms and led her hands to her breasts, kneading his own over hers.

He broke the kiss to whisper, his voice gravelly to his own ears, "I am going to be occupied for a bit. Will yeh take care of these for me?"

Sirin nibbled his lip and nodded, sucking to keep him there longer.

Berne nearly stayed, the suction on his lip pulsed in time with his cock, but he knew he only had one chance for their first time. Sirin was considering him as a true match, more than just a farce, and he wanted to show her what a good mate he would be. He wanted her to know he would always see to her pleasure. Hoped somehow he could show her what a gift she was to him.

He was, if nothing, a determined bear, single-minded in his dedication to a task. He'd win her over with his fervor. He'd addled her mind, wringing her pleasure from her so thoroughly that she couldn't possibly regret this, regret him.

Chapter Eleven

Sirin

IN WHICH SIRIN CONDUCTS
FURTHER EXPERIMENTATION,
PRODUCES CONSIDERABLE
RESULTS, FINDS IT TO HER
SATISFACTION, AND IS IN WANT
OF A CHAMBERPOT

SIRIN PLUCKED AT HER nipples, tugging them desperately while Berne kissed down her torso with agonizing slowness. She was not inexperienced by any means, but her past liaisons had been rushed, furtive things. Lunologists could see to their own pleasure quickly and easily. So the people she'd slept with, regardless of gender, in the past had often expected her to augment her pleasure that way, as they surely had been doing for themselves. This though felt entirely different. Berne showed no intention of rushing, no inclination toward hurrying her along, and no proclivity she had any responsibility to see to her own pleasure in that moment. It touched something vulnerable in her. A deep, fragile, hidden portion of her she'd convinced herself had no place in her life.

She'd always been too caught up in research for relationships. Needing to travel so frequently, tracking down a book or an artifact, she couldn't be tied down permanently. She had plenty of friends—*acquaintances really*—that she could fuck when in town, several of whom had settled down together and were always up for group play, but she'd never had anyone so focused on *her*.

It was a heady thing, being important to someone, being tied to someone. It was intoxicating knowing that as far in the future as she lived, she would wake up in a bed smelling of him. And eventually, there would be someone who knew her body nearly as well as she did.

On his way to her cunt, Berne stopped to nurse at her bite mark, which might as well have been her clit for the waves of pleasure it sparked. She hadn't had time, or the lunula, to investigate what was happening to her body there, but it was something more than a regular scar. For now, all that mattered was that it somehow had a direct connection to her cunt, and she wouldn't argue or question it. He caressed her soft belly, tickling her lightly with his beard before he moved his hands back to her pussy.

Splayed before him, Berne paused, staring at her. Embarrassment rose on her face. No one had ever *looked* at her there beyond whatever was needed to locate it. He stared, his face hungry and she couldn't imagine why he wasn't *doing* anything. After a few moments of this, she cleared her throat. "This is rather intimate," she said awkwardly, "you can just dive in, or come inside; I'm ready enough."

He slowly raised his eyes to hers and scoffed. "Ready *enough?* I don't think so." The corner of his mouth quirked. "And *of course* it's intimate, I'm learning you. It feels important, like I need to. Like if I look long enough, I might see who yeh are. Is that alright?"

Berne's eyes roamed leisurely across her sex as he worked his lips intently with his teeth and tongue. He flushed, the pinkness of his skin a stark contrast to his white beard and hair. After a few moments, he drew back one hand to stroke his beard, smiling as his tongue darted to lick his lip. His other trailed along each of her folds, teasing the edges of her. He spread her slickness up over the expanse of her clit, causing her to gasp.

Sirin felt as if he'd knocked her on her ass. Berne's intense attention was overwhelming, disorienting and disarming her. He was

burrowing into her, and he hadn't even breached
her yet. That he *wanted* to see who she was,
and he felt this was the way to achieve that was
stunning to her. It made tears prick at the edges
of her eyes. While she still felt like squirming
under his intense gaze, his reasoning touched her
heart. Biting her lips and slowed her tugging on her
breasts. Her arousal had calmed to a low simmer
in her discomfort. After a few moments, she found
she was at peace with his gaze.

He was so intent on her that she, in turn,
got to stare shamelessly at him. His breathing
quickened, and for a moment, he looked every
inch a hungry bear eyeing his meal. With that
same methodical determination, he massaged her,
lowering his mouth closer as if drawn by a
lodestone.

His arousal increased her own, and Sirin felt
it drip down her swollen center, begging for his
mouth. When he raised his eyes back to her, his
voice cracked, deeper than normal.

"May I taste yeh?" he rumbled. She nodded,
breathless and dazed in the aftermath of his
perusal.

Sirin gasped when he nudged her mound with
his nose and licked a wide swath across her
opening, humming his enjoyment. She blushed, for
some reason inordinately grateful he was pleased
with her. He lifted her legs, draping them over

his shoulders. Grasping onto her thighs, he lapped at the edges of her entrance, sucking her labia into his mouth with the prickle of his mustache. Berne lavished attention on the lip that had always been longer, sucking and toying with it inside his mouth, transforming something she'd always been self-conscious about into a feature. She'd never bothered to modify it because it had seemed a betrayal of her body, and who would ever really notice anyhow? Now, she was infinitely grateful she'd not done so because it would have been such a waste to miss the blissful sensation.

Berne's noises of pleasure removed any doubts she had about whether this was merely a perfunctory exercise for him. This was for his enjoyment as much as hers. His careful exploration *finally* led him to her clitoris and she cried out, shoving her fist in her mouth. He chuckled against her, the vibration buzzing through her.

"There's no need to be quiet, no neighbors to speak of, and I built the place solid. No one will hear yeh," he reassured.

Suddenly, the thought, the image of him building this place, sweating and shirtless, flashed into her mind, making her groan.

Had he built the walls thick with this exact purpose in mind? She wondered. *Did he build them thick so someday he could hear his wife scream without anxiety?*

The thought he'd been thinking of her, planning to pleasure her this way for years, was delicious. Truly, it didn't matter one way or the other, but the thought spurred her on, driving her toward the precipice of her orgasm. Berne licked up each side of the hood of her clit, avoiding the sensitive top. He circled down and around, flicking his tongue along the underside. She dug her hands into his curls as she filled the house with her cries.

"Oh, Goddess Berne!" she cried. "Oh please—so good!"

Sirin's breath sped as he pulsed the flat side of his tongue against her, and her words devolved into a blubbering mess of screams and pleas. He hummed against her core and lifted her hips to him, following her rhythm.

Every so often, he would thrash his head from side to side, like he was attempting to dig his way deeper into her. The motion was so damn erotic, like his craving for her drove him to consume her. As her breath quickened, the feeling inside her boiled. He whispered encouragements she could barely hear but could *feel* against her cunt. When she felt as if she could take the sweet torture no longer, Berne sealed his mouth around her clit, sucking enough to make her release loud huffing pants as her orgasm ripped through her, wiping all thoughts from her mind. Sirin shattered under the force of it, briefly disconnected from the world entirely, existing as nothing more than the feeling of her cunt contracting and the ripples of pleasure they released.

As her orgasm faded, the stimulation became entirely too intense, and she wiggled back away from him, sputtering gibberish and flailing her legs off of his shoulders. He pulled back with a chuckle and licked his lips. Closing his eyes as he savored the taste of her on his mouth. She felt boneless, wrecked by the strongest orgasm she'd had in years. Not to mention, certainly the only one she'd had without magical augmentation in even longer. She couldn't remember ever having a more intense experience. *Though*, she allowed, *my brain does feel like soup right now.*

He pushed away from the bed, standing above her, eyes half-lidded as his hands traveled to his belt.

His expression shifted as his smug smile fell from his face and his eyes widened in uncertainty. Berne's face shuttered as he asked, "Was that alright? Would yeh like to be done?" he looked suddenly unsure. "We don't have to—"

Sirin let out a sound of outrage. "Alright? That was *fucking* fantastic, and if you think you're going to wind me up like that and then ask if I need to be done, you're sorely underestimating me. What I would *like*," she said with a smirk, "is for you to be naked so I can play with you. Is *that* alright?"

He blushed and unbuckled his belt, dropping his pants to the floor, refusing to meet her eyes.

She giggled, sat up and grabbed his hand, warm and rough in hers. Yanking him forward, he tumbled onto the bed with a grunt.

"Oh," she teased, drawing out the word. "Who's blushing now? You got your turn, so now it's my turn to explore, *sir*." She pushed him onto his back. He groaned and closed his eyes before looking down at her with such tortured anticipation that it stung her heart. Sirin tenderly trailed her hands down his thick torso, savoring the tantalizing sight of him. Berne was solid in every sense of the word, thick and long and weeping with arousal.

She dragged her fingers through the tight white curls that wreathed his swollen length, before trailing her fingers over the silky skin. The vulnerability of the moment struck her, the texture of his skin speaking of something worth earning and cherishing.

Her arousal sat heavily between her thighs, but more powerful was the familiar feeling of curiosity driving her toward discovery. A deep desire, a need, to map him out. To immerse herself in the feel and touch and smell and taste of him. She gripped his length, pulling back his foreskin to reveal the glistening, maroon head. Berne hissed in pleasure, and Sirin savored the sound as it sizzled through her. His wetness called to her, and she allowed herself the luxury of lapping the beads seeping from his slit. She rubbed the softness of his length along her cheeks and chin, enjoying his heat and the slide of his arousal on her face.

Further, Sirin mused, she loved his tortured look, eyes screwed shut as he tried not to move. She gripped him firmly around the base of his cock and gave a solid squeeze. Berne's hips bucked, his control slipping. She smiled smugly, savoring the feeling of power as she watched him writhe beneath her. Berne panted as she pulled upwards on his shaft to cover his head, his foreskin begging to be tasted. She bent and sucked it into her mouth, enjoying its softness and extensibility. She slipped her tongue between foreskin and glans, and he released a surprised grunt. Sirin giggled and retracted his skin, circling his head with her tongue.

"Sirin—" he called, voice taut with tension.

"Mmmm?" she hummed.

"I don't know how long I can—it's been a while and I just don't ken how long I can last if yeh keep—" he gasped as she sucked hard on his head, taking as much of his length into her mouth as she could. She dragged her tongue along the underside of his cock, caressing the thick vein he had there. Sirin increased her suction and came off the top of his head with a pop before wiping a thick string of viscous liquid off of her bottom lip.

"Too much?" She smirked.

"Just a bit. I *am* trying to let yeh play, woman. But I think yeh are determined to kill me instead," he whined, hips fucking into her hand. "I am trying to let yeh have your fun, but we might have to come back to this."

"*Oh*?" She lowered her head to lick him from base to tip, never looking away from his strained face. "I simply thought if we were exploring then—" She cut off and giggled as he surged up to flip her onto her back.

"I am telling yeh, *wife*, I can't take much more, and I'm trying real hard to be impressive." He nuzzled between her breasts and ran a hand along her slit. "Now, unless yeh have objections, I'm going to fill this pretty pussy, and yeh can return to your special brand of torture later."

"Well, I suppose," Sirin said with feigned annoyance. "You'll find I don't take kindly to interruptions in my research, and I was finding you to be such an interesting subject. But, I *suppose*, as long as it promises to be diverting..." Sirin raised her eyebrows at him, her breath catching as he fit his length along her slit.

"Diverting? Aye, I'll show yeh diverting," he taunted back, his grin wicked. Berne slid himself along her folds, gliding along her clit, and coated his cock in her slickness. Sirin moaned and he kissed her deeply, the taste of her own arousal lingering on his tongue, tart and earthy.

Finally, Berne notched his blunt head at her entrance and pressed firmly inside, slow despite her slickness. He worked himself deeper with shallow thrusts, opening her wide, molding her channel until he filled her, until his pelvis ground against her own. He tipped his forehead to hers and they froze, panting. Sirin wrapped her legs around his waist, pressing into his back and grinding her cunt against him.

"Berne," she gasped, feeling his hardness jump inside her. "You're *everywhere!*" And he was. Like she'd been made for him, or he for her, they fit and locked together. Two pieces of a puzzle finally reunited. It was too much, too perfect. She was raw before him, overcome by the overwhelming, consuming.

No, that was ridiculous. One did *not* fall in love in a day. They just didn't; it was categorically impossible. But yet, there was *something*. A seed, a spark she'd never felt. A connection that could easily grow into love.

Sirin stared into his deep blue eyes, terrified and overjoyed and unmoored and so, so *relieved.* This was a person she could *love*, who could love her. He looked at her with such sincere adoration. Had cracked her open so completely before him that her every nerve felt on fire with the feel of him.

With slow, deliberate relentlessness, he withdrew and drove into her again, his rhythm teasing and torturous. She whined, and the sound seemed to release something within him. Berne growled and rose on his knees, pulling her onto his lap. The change made it so he was deeper, and she gasped as she canted her hips against his. Sirin's inner walls throbbed, her world narrowing to where he entered her, where his hands clutched her thighs, his heavy-lidded gaze captivating her. He released one of his hands to caress her belly and pressed his large thumb over her clit. The fire raging in her cunt shot up and ricocheted in her brain, her orgasm making her cry out as her muscles clenched around him. She fell off the precipice of her pleasure, tingling with ecstasy, toes curled and back arched.

Vaguely, she was aware when Berne lost all semblance of composure as she came, roaring and pumping into her before rising onto his knees and holding her firmly against him as he came. As he came down from his orgasm, he pumped a few more times and rubbed her thighs.

He let her legs fall to the bed and she wiped her hair away from her eyes. Berne shivered and lay over her, burrowing into her neck and kissing it gently. They lay quietly, running their hands over one another and soaking in the moment as their breaths calmed. After a pause, Berne looked around the room before he chuckled and buried his head in her shoulder, laughing.

"What?" Sirin asked, suddenly self-conscious. Had that not been as good for him as it had for her?

"I didn't think to grab anything to clean up with. I don't love sleeping in a wet spot, so I suppose I'll need to figure something out. Someone, *me*, a while ago apparently, thought throwing my shirt across the room was a good idea, but it would be pretty handy right now."

Sirin burst out laughing with him. She smacked his shoulder playfully.

"I thought there was something wrong, I thought—" she cut off her voice devolved into a whisper "I thought you didn't have a good time." Mortification heated her face. It'd *seemed* like he'd enjoyed himself, but he might have been regretting saddling himself with her for a partner. Intensely grateful and so overcome with the magnitude of feeling swelling in her breast, Sirin leaned into the side of Berne's face. She pursed her lips against his temple and breathed in sharply.

"Did yeh just smell me?" he asked, his eyes crinkling in mirth.

Sirin blushed; she hadn't even thought about doing it. It had been a purely instinctual action, one she'd not engaged in since being home. Tears formed at the corners of her eyes, and she cleared her throat, smiling. "It's actually a cultural thing. I am honestly not sure why we do it. It's a closeness thing. For loved ones." She shrugged, trying to play it off. If he thought it was weird, it was not like she needed to keep doing it—though even thinking of that felt like a rejection.

Berne leaned up to kiss her on her forehead, and he sniffed in as he did so. "I love that. Did I do it right?"

Sirin pressed her lips together, nodding. "That was just right."

"When I said yeh were a gift, I had no idea." He looked down at her before softly kissing her lips, cheeks, and eyelids. "I'm the happiest, proudest man in the world because I get to do that over and over again for the rest of my life." He squeezed her close, trailing his fingers down her spine.

"Really?" she asked, knowing that she was moon-eyed after his lovely words. "You aren't disappointed you ended up with me?"

The deep rumble of his laughter vibrated through her as he ducked his face into her neck. "Never! If I'm disappointed in anything, it's in myself. I wanted to make this perfect and I'm realizing I have nothing to catch my seed, nowhere inside for yeh to pee, and I didn't start a fire before we started and yeh might be getting cold," he punctuated his sentences with kisses.

"Oh well, I am pretty cozy right now," she said, wiggling beneath him.

"Good, it's a start. Because I still feel like I need to trick yeh into being happy with me and I'm worried I haven't done enough. I know yeh didn't have much choice in the matter but I'd prefer it not be something yeh regret forever. I *will* be a good mate to yeh Sirin and I swear I'll show yeh every day how grateful I am to hav yeh," he smiled and tucked his head back into the crook of her neck. "Plus, I'll take yeh to see where the lady sleeps tomorrow, and that has to count for something eh?"

Sirin nodded and thought for a moment before scratching into his beard. "I haven't had much time to process, but I can think of thousands of worse scenarios than to be stuck in the exact place I need to be to do my research with an insanely handsome man who gives me the *most delicious* sex I have ever had." She cupped his face, rubbing her thumb along his temple. "You didn't choose this either. But I don't want you thinking for the next seventy years you need to make this up to me. You saved my life and got an, admittedly gorgeous, talented, kind, wonderful, sexy wife out of it."

He nodded into her neck and she laughed at herself. "But seriously, we're partners now, which means we're equal, alright?"

"Alright," he said before whispering into her shoulder, "but I can still be very grateful I got to save yeh, out of anyone else in the world. I have it on very good authority yeh are smart, talented, and kind."

"Hey!" She laughed. "And gorgeous and sexy and...something else!"

"Oh no, love," he whispered against her ear. "I don't need to know those things second hand. I trust my own judgment that you're *the most* gorgeous and sexy far more than yours."

Tears stung her eyes as Berne pushed himself off of her and cupped his cock in his hand before lunging for his shirt. He wadded it up and shoved it between her legs. "Hold that, I will be right back." Once his pants were back on, he kissed her lightly and moved toward the door.

"Where are you going?" she called after him, bewildered.

"I'm getting yeh a chamberpot from somewhere so yeh can pee inside!"[1] He winked at her and shut the door. Sirin burst out laughing, marveling at her fortune. This morning, she'd been convinced she was getting close to finding something she'd looked for her entire life. She'd had no idea she would find it and something far more precious than she'd ever imagined.

---

1. I am happy to report we installed a flush toilet shortly thereafter.

Chapter Twelve

Berne

IN WHICH NEW
ACQUAINTANCES ARE MADE,
BERNE'S TRAINING BEGINS IN
EARNEST—PROVING A STIFF
PUPIL—AND EQUIPMENT IS
ORDERED

SIRIN WAS… A MARVEL.

The following morning, she flitted about the town, notebook in hand, interviewing people and taking notes on each people's preferences and customs. She carefully recorded which groups had specific greetings and food requirements, and noted which people showed a specific interest or aptitude she wanted to explore. He'd trailed behind her, arms steadily filling with welcome gifts from her growing pack of admirers. He knew he looked a love-sick fool, but he hadn't ever felt so happy.

She'd left her vest at home and carefully dressed similar to other women in the village, rolling her sleeves up past her elbows and allowing the top buttons of her shirt to remain open. Upon seeing many of the women didn't fret about tying their hair back, Sirin had gleefully freed hers from her braid.

"Where I was born, on an island off the coast of the mainland, we only wore our hair loose when we were young but all of our bodices had big, poofy shorter sleeves which would let the air in to cool us," she said. "This reminds me of that." She smiled at him wistfully, like it was a secret between them. "Makes me feel like this is really my home."

Berne cupped her cheek, rubbing it with his thumb. "I'm glad," he whispered. "I want yeh to feel like this is your home as much as mine. When we get your new clothes made, yeh should tell them to make some with big sleeves like that."[1]

"I'd like that. I have a few dresses that might—" She gasped when a young centaur girl walked by them. Sirin held up a finger and went running off to meet her. On the way, she tripped, grinding

---

1. After spending years living in a society that expected me to erase any vestiges of my own culture, being with Berne was a revelation. He valued the parts of me that I'd hidden for years and went out of his way to embrace them in our life.

her knees and skirt into the grass. Berne's heart skipped in panic as he leaped to catch her, but she was too far. She stood up, wincing, before Berne could even arrive. He realized then, how vulnerable he was to her, how much he was already beginning to care. His feelings were quickly solidifying into something like love, and he liked how Sirin seemed to need him.

Sirin was asking the young centaur—Maerin—for a drawing when Berne joined them. The young girl agreed, she'd only been off to see a friend and didn't mind the delay, and Sirin sat on the grass, motioning for Berne to sit too.

Her remarkably lifelike sketches made him notice things about people he had never even thought to pay attention to. Before her sketch of the young centaur, he hadn't given a second thought to the fact that the hair on their heads did not match that of their bodies. Like everyone in Sanctuary, they had white hair on their heads, but their bodies had any number of equine colorings.

As Sirin sketched, he leaned close and whispered in her ear, gratified to see her shiver at his closeness. "I'd like yeh to try to be more careful with yourself. Rushing about like that all the time is going to get yeh hurt."

"Oh hush," she whispered back, entirely focused on her notebook. "My hastiness doesn't hurt anyone but myself. If I get injured it's not like it would affect anyone but me."

Berne put a hand under her chin. "When yeh were hurt was one of the worst things I've ever experienced and yeh weren't even properly mine yet. I only have the one wife yeh see, and I'll not respond well to her being injured."

She turned her face to his, and he was drunk on those big, deep eyes. She blinked several times, and he thought there might have been liquid pooling along her lower lid as she nodded. He tucked some of her hair behind her ear as she whispered, "Alright."

He was pleased to see other people were as taken with her as he'd been. That others were also swept up in her special brand of excitement, pulled along by the current of her enthusiasm.

Shortly after the sketch was finished, one of the young finfolk boys, Sigfinn, Berne thought, leaped out of the water and introduced himself to her, ignoring Berne entirely. Berne walked behind them, chuckling at Sirin as she tried to downplay her surprise. Her dark eyes flitted all over the boy's blue-scaled skin, webbed hands and feet, and large eyes. She tilted her head to the side and pursed her lips. Was she trying to determine if Sig had gills? She raised her eyebrows, a gleeful look crossing her face before she turned her attention back to what the boy was saying. Without looking down, she scribbled something in her notebook and snapped it shut.

"...and yeh know, I live in the river and the canals, so I can get as much lunula as yeh need. We could get special dispensation if we needed samples from the Lady's lake!" Sigfinn was bouncing on his toes, his eye ridges raised with hope.

Sirin smiled at the boy. Good Lady, she was beautiful when she smiled. "I would love to have help—if you think you can get away from your studies..." She trailed off, her eyes questioning.

"Oh, um, actually," Sigfinn said, his face blushing purple. "I am at the point where I'm ready to apprentice, and I know it's sudden, but I thought I might ask you. I've been trying to figure out where I could apprentice for weeks now and nothing has felt right, yeh know?"

Sirin nodded. "I do. I could certainly use an assistant, but I don't know if I will have the funds to pay for an apprenticeship. I haven't nearly gotten that far yet." Sigfinn's face fell and his eyes dropped to the ground. Sirin grabbed his arm and continued. "But if we can get that worked out, then I would be happy to entertain your bid. For reference, do you have any school work you could show me that demonstrates your writing ability, scientific knowledge, especially chemistry and biology, and perhaps your artistic aptitude?"

Sigfinn's smiled broadly, his pointed teeth taking up half of his face. "Oh yes, those were my favorites!" he said. "I have a paper on the hybridization of the winged lynx that might work!"

Sirin smiled and squeezed the boy's hand. "I think that will do fine! Would you bring it by tomorrow, along with a guardian? I am still settling in, so I am afraid I am a bit out of sorts just now."

Sigfinn shook her hand enthusiastically and dove into the canal with a wave. Sirin turned back to Berne with an adorable frown.

"He is the cutest and damn charming, too!" she said, flinging her hand over her heart and tucking herself into Berne's side.

Berne pulled her into a hug, amazed at how *easy* everything felt already. It likely helped that Sirin was very comfortable with physical affection. He tilted to look down at her. Her cheeks were flushed, making her seem to glow in the sunlight. Sweat-dampened strands framed her face as she smiled at him before rising on toes to kiss his nose.

"Do I need to worry about losing yeh to a wee fish boy?" he joked.

Sirin nudged him with her shoulder and scoffed. "He's much too young... now if there is a fish Daddy around here..." she teased, raising her brows and pretending to look around.

Berne swatted her lightly on her voluptuous ass, following it with a squeeze. "There are not, I am afraid. All of the fish Daddies, as yeh say, have fled the area. There are reports of predatory southern women in the village," he said gravely. "And such women need things like bears to keep 'em in line, so it is. They'd walk all over a poor wee fish Daddy." Berne pretended to scoff as Sirin collapsed against him, giggling. "Yeh laugh, but it's my *duty* to protect the people of this village from dangerous outsiders who might exploit them!"

Sirin gasped, grabbing onto him and looking comically around. "Where? We've got to get you out of here; if they are looking for attractive men, you are in danger!"

"Ach, I'll have yeh know, I have sacrificed myself to one such woman, in hopes we can stem the tide," he said. Sirin nodded back up at him, a smirk sneaking through her attempts at a serious expression.

"Truly sir, you are the most selfless guard in all of Sanctuary," she whispered, as if in awe.

Berne laughed. "Most selfish, more like! Oh no, help! I'm stuck with a beautiful woman! My life is well and truly over," he teased before bending to kiss her properly. He slipped his tongue between her lips and the bright taste of berries burst on his tongue. He was selfish, but he was happy to be so. He could already see how she would fit in here, how much life and thirst for knowledge she would bring to them all. As he moved to deepen the kiss, he felt familiar small hands grasp at fistfuls of his pants.

"Stop goggin her Uncy!" said Ursule's voice from behind him.

"It's *hoggin,* Suley," Ingrid corrected from the other side.

Berne pulled back from their kiss and cleared his throat. "Sirin, I would like to introduce yeh to the most important little girls in my world. This is Ursule," he said, turning to the side so Sirin could see the girls. "And that there is Ingrid, my nieces."

Sirin gasped, as he suspected she would. The girls were half-orc, so while they had the same white hair as he and their mother, their skin was a pale mossy green, and their ears were delicately pointed. He pressed his lips together, attempting to hide his amusement; the girls' dresses were covered in mud from the waist down, and their hair was full of twigs and leaves.

"I thought we was the most important girls, not the most important *little* girls!" Ingrid said, crossing her arms.

"Well, girls, yeh see, when yeh have a mate, they have to be your favorite *big* person, but you'll always be my little favorites. Now, can yeh do your nice introductions, please?"

The girls nodded, though Ingrid looked a bit grumpy, and held out their tiny hands to shake Sirin's.

"It really is lovely to meet you," she said. "And I have *no* favorite girls at the moment. Would you two be interested in the job?"

The girls giggled as he spotted Catrin behind them, tying up their rowboat. She jogged over, waving to Sirin. "It's nice to meet you! I came by yesterday, but yeh were asleep. I'm Catrin," she said with a wave. " I was hoping yeh both might consider joining us for supper tonight. Mom and Dad can come too, so yeh can meet all of us!" Catrin looked at Sirin hopefully.

"If we don't have any other plans...—" Sirin looked at Berne.

"No, we don't. What should we bring?" he asked, though he mouthed "Honey cakes," at the same moment she said it aloud.

They chatted with Catrin and the girls for a while, but Berne stiffened when he spotted Gunna approaching. Catrin raised her eyebrows cheekily. "Oh, gosh, I just remembered we need to go talk to Mrs. Swensen about her order! Look at the time, have a great day yeh lovebirds!" she said.

Berne frowned as she scurried away, herding the girls before her as they blew kisses around her legs. He turned to Sirin to reassure her. With Gunna walking straight for them, Sirin was sure to feel nervous. Instead, when he looked down at her, Sirin's eyes were alight with glee and she was smiling maniacally.

"Are yeh alright?" he asked under his breath. "Yeh look a wee bit deranged. I know Gunna can be intimidating but—"

"Berne, dear," Sirin whispered between the clenched teeth of her smile, "this woman couldn't scare me if she tried. Don't worry about me. I love this shit. Your job is to keep a straight face and look supportive. Deal?"

"Uh, if yeh say so," he answered skeptically. Berne was positively fascinated with his new mate. She was constantly surprising him and he chuckled at the thought he had felt he'd known her after watching her for a week. Something told him he wouldn't really know her for years.

"Ah, here is our hasty bear and his wily researcher," Gunna said as she approached. She held her thin hands clasped in front of her, her head snapping between them with sharp movements.

"Hello, Head Councillor, lovely day, isn't it? How can we help you? Berne has been showing me around your lovely village," Sirin said.

"Indeed," Gunna replied. "I have come to inform yeh that yeh can expect instruction daily from just after noon until five o'clock. We expect yeh to complete the entire curriculum for our schooling system, and only once it's done will you'll be assigned a workspace.[2] Further, the council will schedule a meeting where we can discuss the direction of your research and guidelines for any writings yeh complete."

Berne looked between the two women. If it were him, he'd be swatting the ground with his paws in defense. He was nearly ready to do so for Sirin. He acknowledged he was already popping his jaw, which Gunna noticed, and shot him a quelling look. He lowered his head into his shoulders in deference. He'd stood up to Gunna a great deal over the last few days, and it seemed she wasn't going to stand for more.

Berne looked to Sirin, who was watching the exchange with a puzzled look. It occurred to him his new wife wasn't used to people communicating in postures like this. He'd need to show her. She squeezed his hand and turned back to Gunna.

"Sounds lovely. I look forward to learning the curriculum and seeing the space. I have at least one individual interested in assisting in my research. Please let me know if you think of anyone else. Further, I have a bit of money in the currency of the Compact; is there any way of changing that over? I

---

2. I'll be a bit of a braggart and say that I completed said curriculum within six weeks, it helped that I really only needed to learn those things specific to Sanctuary but it went faster than otherwise since those things were exceedingly fascinating to me. By eight weeks, Sigfinn and I were immersed in our research.

would like to be able to pay the individuals working for me, thank you!" Sirin said sweetly.

Gunna blinked and Berne suppressed a chuckle. No, his wife didn't need his help at all, it seemed. Gunna cleared her throat. "Actually, we use the same currency. Our Lady established it across Timonde prior to her slumber, so the value may be different than what yeh expect, but it should work fine. Our outrunners have spent ours with little trouble at outposts in the past." Gunna straightened her shoulders and cocked her head. "I do believe that will be all, thank yeh Mr. and Mrs. Brodersen–Agbuya. Good day." Gunna nodded curtly and strode away from them.

Berne turned to Sirin, wide–eyed. She'd handled Gunna better than he *ever* had, though she'd never been caught pilfering from Gunna's berry bushes.

Sirin smiled up at him, her joy spread across her face. After a moment, she widened her eyes in surprise and bit her lip. Dear Lady, she was the prettiest thing he had ever seen.

That one small motion shot straight through him, reminding him of private nibbles and her looking up at him through her lashes. He breathed in through his nose. The middle of town, right next to one of the most heavily traveled canals, was *not* the place to get a hard–on. No matter how gorgeous or sexy she was when she was demanding.

Sirin went onto her tiptoes and kissed him on the cheek. "You know, you can use lunula to deal with that, Mr. Brodersen–Agbuya," she whispered as she grasped his cock through his pants. Berne could feel a blush color his cheeks and he let out some sort of ridiculous sound as she squeezed. "It's like you people spend so much of your energy and lunula on shifting that you forget everything else you can do with it."

Berne nodded, like the idiot he was. He wasn't practiced at using lunula in such ways, or consciously at all. So much of how he used lunula was instinctual that he almost never thought to use it consciously. Berne's shoulders tensed, and he looked around to see if anyone was watching them. They were in public, but it seemed for the moment no one was *staring* at them, at him. He closed his eyes and drew in a shuddering breath when he saw they were completely alone, her hand stroking his arm.

"There," she whispered. "Imagine your body is a river, the whole thing connected to the Spine. Each vein is a tributary connecting you to the magic that runs through you. Visualize it, *feel* it coursing through you. All over your body, it's working to make changes, to keep you healthy. I want you to follow the branch that leads to your penis."

For a moment, the clinical use of the word startled Berne; he almost never called it that. But, he could see she used it intentionally, clinically, so he could focus.

When she spoke again, he could feel the smile in her voice. "Have you found it?" He nodded as he located it. He had never before thought of it in this way; it had always been part of who he was, but picturing it this way was smooth, easy.

"I want you to direct some of that stream to leave. You should be able to tell the amount," she whispered. And sure enough, he could *feel* the amount of blood he needed for normal functioning, and the extra blood that engorged him. He wasn't sure, at first, how he should "direct" it, but like so much of how he currently used it, the lunula seemed to respond to his gentle *suggestion* to move that amount of blood out of his cock.

"That's so, so good," Sirin said, and he could *swear* she was trying to be sexy. Her voice was lowered, only for him, and there was a rasp to it he had only heard in the bedroom. A second later, she grabbed at his cock again and the blood tried to rush back. "Ah, ah, ah. Keep it out of there. You can do this, just shunt it somewhere else, it doesn't need to be there right now."

She punctuated her phrases with tugs, making stemming the flow of blood back into his cock damn near impossible.

"Lass," he grunted, "I don't ken how yeh think I am gonna manage it with yeh yanking on the thing like you're trying to harvest a damn carrot."

Sirin giggled but gave him a firm tug, milking a grunt out of him before releasing him. He didn't know if he felt grateful or disappointed, but surely it was both. She gave him one last pat, and *finally* he felt like he was able to return things to normal. *This woman is going to kill me, but I just might die happily.*[3]

Berne cleared his throat and tried not to blush even further when he looked down at Sirin's smug face. He grabbed her hand before she could accost him again and started leading her toward Seam Square. He could *feel* the glee radiating off of her, the infernal woman.

"C'mon," he said, "there's lots more to see and do, first we need to get your measurements on file with the clothiers, then we should see about getting yeh a chair."

---

3. Because the people of Sanctuary are such astoundingly powerful lunologists, they often don't actively think about how they are using it. Most of their effects happen entirely subconsciously and I have found, as a result, that shifting this mindset to more active control is difficult at first. Berne's body wasn't actually interested in not being hard, since he was receiving tactile feedback. Going against his body's natural instincts was difficult, whereas working with their bodies, they tend to be extremely successful. Most often, the human shifters of Sanctuary don't even realize they are catching a cold, since their body heals it before they even notice.

"Clothes and chairs are very nice, but what I'd really like is a glass blower," Sirin said.

"A glass blower?" Berne asked. "Why would yeh need one of them?"

"To set up my laboratory. I have a whole list of glassware I will need. Plus I suppose I need to find out if what I have on hand for money will be enough. If not, I might need to give you a letter of withdrawal for my account for the next time you go into Pershing. I'll also need cleaning products and some specific chemicals. Oh damn, I am not sure you are going to have iodine on hand. Do you all have iodine?" Sirin said.

Adorable, Berne decided. Adorable was the perfect word for her. "Of course, if that's what yeh need, we'll see it done. Gunna might be showing a hard face, but the council knows we need your research. We don't think of lunula in the same way yeh do. We don't use it the same, not like you. We start so young, it's not something we think about really, we jus' do it."

"I noticed," she said. "When do you all start? On average, I mean."

"Honestly, I'm not sure. I'm fair certain the girls have been for a while now. They had a bit, a month or so ago, where they kept cutting their hair to grow it back out." He scratched his beard. He knew they must do it other times, but honestly couldn't think of anything. "Often, it's just we're especially healthy, so it's hard to notice. Learning to shift is a long process, but none of it is explained in your type of scientific terms. It's all meditation and communing and the like."

"Interesting. Well, we'll work on your control yet," Sirin said with a sly smile, her hand just *happening* to graze the front of his trousers. "You know," she continued with a thoughtful look, "a cage might help you with that. We could look into it."

Berne gulped. "A cage? What do yeh mean a cage?"

"For your cock. I think it would help you learn to manually control your blood flow if you had tactile feedback," she said as if suggesting they buy him a new shirt.

Berne felt the blood drain from his face. That sounded *horrible*. Why would she even suggest such—

"Mmmm, I see," Sirin said. "Looks like that's probably a hard limit then!" She stood on her tiptoes to kiss him. "No worries! I don't want to torture you into learning! I have some other ideas anyhow! Now how about those measurements? And do we need to pick up anything for this cake? I want to get to the glassmith as quickly as we can! I have a list here in my notebook, but can they read common?"

Berne shook his head, she was taking to everything like a bear cub to snow. She was excitable, overwhelming, and talked faster than he could think half the time. He couldn't have designed himself a better mate.

"Yes, lass, let's go see about your glass. We can always get measurements and groceries after," he said. Sirin squealed and ran off toward the center of town, her body undulating in a way that forced him to practice his lunology again. He ran after her chuckling. Considering she didn't know where to find the glassmith, he wasn't sure where she thought she was going. What he was sure of, though, was he'd be happy to follow regardless.

Chapter Thirteen
EPILOGUE

IN WHICH ALL PREVIOUSLY AFOREMENTIONED, BUT AS OF YET UNSATISFIED PROMISES ARE FULFILLED

T WO MONTHS LATER

"She looks so young," Sirin whispered, afraid to wake the sleeping Goddess floating in the deep pool under the mountain.

"She does. Thought she'd be a grown lady," Berne replied. They looked over a ledge, gripping the handrail a hundred feet above. Their whispers echoed through the large cavern, punctuated by drips of condensation off the stalactites. "At least she's big. I think I would be more disappointed if our Lady was normal-sized."

Sirin chuckled. "I imagine she can be any size she likes, love."

She stared in wonder as the currents brought lunula close to the Goddess, and lit up as it became infused with her magic. She'd always imagined there would be some ecological explanation for their magic. It was somewhat embarrassing she'd dismissed the divine origin theories almost immediately. Regardless of her embarrassment, she felt nothing short of utter awe to be both in the presence of her Goddess and to have found the answers, and even more titillating questions, concerning her life's quest.[1]

Sirin was thrilled that knowing the source of magic had only opened more avenues for research. She practically vibrated at the thought of commencing studies on how the people of Sanctuary gained shifting abilities, as well as the ever-changing hybrid animals. Her initial theory was the constant influx of lunula tended to speed up evolution in some ways and made it take a complete left turn in others. Sudden spontaneous mutations seemed common, and hybrids between

---

1. At this point, we have all heard so much about our Goddess, that I don't want to belabor the issue. My assistants and I have published our observations about her periodically, and though they are probably dry, I like to think they are extremely insightful. If dry observations are not your craic (that is why I am writing fictionalized accounts, in fact), She will return in future books.

animals happened often enough that several established species were native to the area. Her new neighbors had shared that hybrids didn't even arise from breeding, per se, but instead from predator-prey relationships. They had several species of winged animals she was fairly certain came from animals consuming birds, cats and foxes chief among them.

Berne shifted to stand behind her, wrapping his thick arms around her waist and plopping his head on her shoulder. It seemed resting his head on her was a favorite position of his, regardless of whether he was shifted into his bear form or not. They stood silently together, enjoying each other's company and the tranquility of the Lady's pool.

"I am not certain we can truly call her a lady," Sirin thought, "she looks to be 16."

After several quiet minutes, Sirin became aware of Berne's hardness pressing into her backside. She giggled quietly and whispered, "I don't know if that is an appropriate form of worship, sir."

"If she didn't want me to worship yeh, she shouldn't have made yeh so tempting. Don't get me wrong, she is majestic and everything, but how long are we gonna stand here and look at her? I have an important appointment with my mate, yeh see."

"Mmmm, I see." Sirin nodded. "That sounds very official. I would hate for you to be late."

"*Oh aye, my mate can be quite cross if she is not regularly attended to. I have to keep a schedule to keep up with her demands! I don't always tell her we have an appointment though; makes it seem spontaneous–like.*"

Sirin ground herself back against him and said, "Well, I would hate to keep her waiting then." She shunted some lunula forward quickly and bolted from the room, hoping he would give chase.

She sprinted back up the tunnel leading down to their Lady's Repose, the echoes of the long hall making it seem as if Berne was right behind her. When she reached the top, she burst through the door, startling the guards, who rolled their eyes at her. Nearly everyone in town was used to their silliness, and the guards seemed no exception. She ran toward a stand of trees as if that would slow him, but truly she wanted the trees to act as a blind for some privacy. Her heart hammered in her chest as she listened for him. She couldn't hear any footfalls, neither two nor four–legged, anywhere around her. The forest seemed silent.

As she stood there, whipping her head around to find him, she suddenly felt the press of his thick cock against her ass again. She turned her head, but couldn't see him there. In fact, she couldn't see anything at all.

"Berne!" she scolded, "What are you playing at?"

Her vision entirely occluded, Sirin was left with nothing but the feel, the scent, and the sounds of him around her. His quick breaths in her ear puffed strands of hair in front of her face and tickled her neck. One hand snaked toward her breasts while the other delved for her rapidly moistening cunt. She squirmed against him, breath catching as he dipped his fingers into her slick folds and plucked at her nipple. He growled in approval and gently nipped at her neck. Sirin squirmed against him and reached back to pull his shirt over his head—that he wasn't wearing?

The soft crackle of fire caused her to open her eyes. The dim lighting revealed the familiar outlines of their home. Behind her, Berne thrust against her and swirled his finger around her clit. The Berne in her bed had merged with the Berne of her dream. Sirin groaned and ground back against the hard bar of his cock, enjoying waking up in her favorite way. She often had no idea who began their midnight sessions, but they were always a welcome surprise. This was especially true since Berne had been away on a long patrol, and she hadn't expected him home until tomorrow.

Sirin's head lolled back onto Berne's shoulder, and she reached back to pull at the hair at the nape of his neck. "Hello, when ah—" He sucked on her mating bite, causing jolts of pleasure to thrum through her body.

"The second I walked in the door, I could smell your arousal, love," he purred against her ear. "I climbed into bed to find yeh wet and wanting; I can't have that now can I?"

Sirin shook her head frantically. Goddess, he knew just how to talk to make her dripping.

Berne's fingers toyed with her, strumming and stoking her desire. Sirin knew his priority was to get her to come, but her cunt felt empty and she wanted him inside her *now*. She could come when he was inside her, simple as that. Sirin bucked against him, grinding against his hardness, feeling him leak a trail of precum between her ass cheeks and up her lower back. Perhaps if she ground enough, turned him on enough, he would relent and fill her up.

Words were increasingly hard to form, but at last, she was able to say what she wanted.

"Berne,—" she gasped, "I—I need, ah—cock, I need your cock!"

Her mate licked a stripe up the side of her neck before sucking on her earlobe and chuckling darkly. "Oh, but I like yeh like this, caught and squirming against me, such good little *prey.*"

Sirin gasped as he shoved his tongue into her ear. Berne *knew* how that reminded her of having him inside of her and he knew how much she loved to be his prey. Her desire spiraled out of control, her breathing turning ragged. She kicked her leg back over his thigh, opening herself to him further.

"I want yeh to come for me, and then, sweetling, I want yeh to *run*," he whispered, voice gravelly with desire.

The second he uttered the words against her ear, Sirin shattered, screaming his name. She convulsed wildly against him as her vision whited out and her awareness reduced to the pleasure he wrung from her, drawing it out with slow pulsing presses of the pad of his finger.

"Yeh have until I clean your slick from my hand before I am coming after yeh," he said, the growl of his bear already creeping into his voice. Sirin jolted from her languid pleasure haze and yelped as she leaped from the bed, ignoring her nightgown hiked above her hips.

She tore open the front door and darted into the night. Berne's shift could be lightning fast when he wanted, so she knew her lead would be short. She turned to run behind the house, it would be predictable, but it would also be private. Most people were sleeping at whatever hour this was, but she knew they weren't likely to be entirely quiet, so she ran for the trees. Her heart pounded in her ears, and her arousal coated the insides of her thighs, making them slide across one another with ease. The cool air bit against her hard nipples, heightening her arousal and the feel of them sliding against her night dress.

When her toes hit the soft blanket of the forest floor, her feet crunching on the sweet needles of pine, Sirin heard their door shut and the galumphing, puffing sound of her bear running her down. She bolted between the trees, branches whipping her face and body, the pain driving her forward. Behind her, she could hear his great body picking up speed. Her heart raced with an adrenaline spike as she dodged around a massive conifer. She knew he would catch her, he always caught her, but she also knew the longer she ran, the more of a chase she gave him, the less control he'd be able to muster when he claimed his prize.

Sirin smiled deviously and dumped some lunula reserves toward speed and reaction time. There was no way she could disguise her trail, by scent or sound, so she didn't bother. Instead, she relied on staying on her feet and running as far and as fast as she could.

The faint green shimmer of the dome glowed up ahead, and she had a choice to make, and quickly. Should she run outside, through the snow, or bank to the side to stay inside the dome? She didn't relish the idea of running in the snow barefoot, but Berne *was* a polar bear. They hadn't yet had sex in the snow and it seemed a shame. Sadly, she wasn't remotely prepared to brave the cold outside, so she turned to run toward the Lady's mountain. She'd dreamt of them in the woods outside, so she might as well embrace it.

Somehow, it seemed Berne had expected her to turn as she could now hear him barreling toward her from the side. She let out a shriek of glee, anticipating what was to come. Sirin never knew if he was going to stay shifted, and it added a delicious suspense to their primal play. Ducking to avoid a branch, Sirin missed Berne's final approach and was entirely surprised when all nine hundred pounds of him tackled her. She let out an "oof" as he barreled into her, using his powerful front paws to wrap her close during their tumble.

After they rolled a few times, Sirin found herself on her back framed on all sides by her massive mate. His paws on either side of her dwarfed her head and she shivered. She loved the exquisite feeling of powerlessness when he was shifted. He could kill her in an instant, she knew, but he would endeavor to drive her mad from pleasure instead.

Not to mention that cock, she smiled deviously. He hadn't yet learned to only partially shift, though she was confident he could do it. She'd found his cock had special *features* when he shifted, and she *wanted* them.

He growled at her, placing one heavy paw on the center of her chest. Then, he snuffed between her legs, and his rhythmic purring began. Hooking one large claw at the top of her nightgown he sliced it down the front, leaving her open to the chill. Berne pulled back, watching her. By this point, she was used to how much her mate enjoyed watching her and she reveled in his attention. Thankfully, Berne loved spoiling *her* with nightdresses as much as he loved spoiling *them*. He licked his enormous teeth and punctuated his purr, so it sounded like a chuckle.

Berne had no appetite for coyness as he lapped at her breasts ruthlessly. The length of his tongue wrapped around each one and toyed with her nipples. He had her panting in no time, and he used his massive paws to roll her over and lift her ass into the air. He steadied her on her knees, and at any moment, she expected to see his large paws on either side of her head as he mounted her.

Instead, Sirin nearly collapsed as Berne thrust the length of his tongue deep inside her pussy. Sirin could feel it writhing within her, twisting to taste and tickle every inch of her cunt. Heat washed over her, the feeling so intense she would have crawled away were it not for his paw holding her in place. After a moment more of delicious torture, he pulled back to lap at her clit. He toyed with her hood, pressing it up to caress her sensitive apex.

"Hah—hah—hah—!" Sirin began making nonsense sounds with each press of his massive tongue. She rocked herself back toward him as he drove her closer to the edge. She would have scrapes on her knees to heal later, but all she could feel was the throb of her pussy and his tongue driving her crazy. The sounds Berne made as a bear were obscene. He couldn't suck her as efficiently in this form, so the clearing they landed in was filled with the slick slurps and rumbles of his enthusiasm. The tension in her body tightened and tightened and Sirin scrabbled her fingers on the ground, clasping at the grass for stability. With each rock against his face, Sirin ground herself against him, desperate for every sensation he could give her. If she wasn't careful, she'd graze one of his massive canines but the sharp bite of pain only heightened her awareness.

Her second orgasm of the night did not take long. The buildup, and the chase, the danger, and his massive tongue had her shattering in moments. She was still riding her high when she felt his hand, human this time, pluck at her nipples, prolonging her pleasure. He slid two thick fingers into her cunt and curled them to massage her G–spot.

"One more. I want one more before I stuff this perfect cunt," he growled behind her.

Sirin whipped her head back and forth, exhausted. She didn't know if she had another in her, but Berne seemed to always think she was capable of "at least one more." He kissed her

back, thrusting and curling his fingers until she
squealed.

"Not only do I think yeh have one more for me,
but I think you'll drench the ground when yeh
do." As he said so, Sirin could feel the pressure
building inside her, the forbidden pleasure she was
only starting to learn to embrace. She whimpered
and nodded her head, she would give him what
he wanted, what she wanted. Her body began
to tingle as her orgasm neared, the tantalizing
and terrifying threshold squeezing in on her. She
screamed into the night as she allowed her release
to overwhelm her, squeezing her eyes against the
onslaught of sensation. Sirin could hear the spray
of her squirt across the grass beneath her before
Berne caught her waist, tugging at her to turn
around.

"You're getting so good at that, my sweet little
prey," he growled, lifting her to him. Berne twined
his hands into her hair and hungrily devoured
her mouth. He demanded her participation with
scrapes of his teeth urging her on despite her
exhaustion. He tortured her and goaded her,
reminding her he was still entirely stimulated,
though she was nearly spent.

Gasping, he pulled back and gently stretched her
languid body on the grass behind him. "I have been
thinking about breeding this gorgeous pussy for
two days now. When I am away, all I can think

of is your taste and the sound of your cries." He pumped one strong hand over his cock and licked his lips. The moon, cutting between trees, glistened on his curling white chest hair. It could be just the afterglow of amazing orgasms, but haloed by the trees and stars, moonlight glinting off a sheen of sweat, Berne looked ethereal. She smiled up at him, infinitely grateful she'd persisted in her quest for answers.

Sirin had imagined having two types of partners in her life. She'd imagined someday she might find a work partner who could help her with her research and encourage her to find better, more accurate answers to her questions. They might pose new questions she'd never thought of before. Or, she'd also considered she might find a partner in life. It was possible she might find someone willing to follow her around and explore her interests. With Berne, she had everything. He might not be incredibly knowledgeable about her area of study, but he was curious and had grown up with knowledge she was only beginning to discover. He was perfect for her.

Berne notched the head of his cock at her entrance and smirked down at her. "What'er you smiling at?"

"I'm thinking how lucky I am—" Sirin replied, cupping his face. "How lucky I am to get to love you," He pressed into her then, making her hiss in pleasure. She wasn't sure she would ever get used to feeling such a perfect cock. She couldn't be certain he *wasn't* changing it with lunula to fill her so completely, but she was not about to complain. Her mate lowered himself to his elbows over her, kissing her on the nose before growling in her ear.

"Now, I am not aiming to fight with yeh when your cunt is squeezing me so sweetly, but I will remind yeh it is me that got lucky in this situation." As soon as he was done speaking, he brought her mating bite to his lips and sucked ruthlessly, nipping and laving at it in ways that made her pussy clench around his length. She'd discovered there were indeed changes that happened with a mating bite. When Berne had cleaned her mating bite with his saliva whilst she was asleep, he'd been modifying the nerves in the area to make them more sensitive and built neural bridges to her medial paracentral lobule, the area of the brain that housed orgasms.

Being a lunologist had allowed her to form a similar bite on his shoulder, which she latched onto with deep sucking pulls. Berne let out a guttural moan and shook his head, trying to resist. They both knew exactly what Sirin wanted, and he might want to stay a man, but Sirin had run into the night to be fucked by a bear.

"Wife," he growled in her ear, both warning and scolding her. "yeh are asking for it."

"Damn right I am," she replied. She bit down on his mate bite and Berne *roared*, unable to contain his bear when he was being goaded so expertly. Inside of her, Sirin felt his cock begin to shift, thickening and changing inside her. There were definite advantages to being fucked by her bear and she wanted them all. His shoulder ripped away from her mouth and she felt a tickle of hair as it sprouted from his skin. In moments, her powerful bear was towering over her, lifting her into the air with his massive paws, spinning her on his length before dropping her to the forest floor once more.

Berne ceased his slow deliberate strokes in favor of frantic slams. Sirin was in no mood, three orgasms in, for slow and sensual. She'd been run down by her bear and she was ready for him to use her for his pleasure. She loved that she was invariably able to send him over the edge by nursing on his bite and she *craved* his abandon when he was usually so in control. His large form completely covered her, enveloping her in his smell. The scent of man and bear that had so intrigued her at the start now made her gush at the thought of him.

She could feel the press of his knot teasing her entrance, the rings that led to his now flared head dragged against her clenching walls, stroking her G–spot.[2] The power he used to plow into her heightened Sirin's arousal, the friction of the forest floor beneath her providing a wonderful counterpoint to the exquisite pull of the ripples of his head inside her. She *needed* him as deep inside of her as possible, so she rocked back on her knees to meet him, driving him on.

Having orgasmed so recently, Sirin was maddeningly sensitive and she was riding the edge of another in short order. She loved all orgasms, but her orgasms when he was inside her were exceptionally mind–shattering. If she could time it right, when he was coming, he would press into her in a way that felt damn near transcendent. She listened to his breathing, trying to gauge when he would be ready. When his claws dug into the ground and he dipped his head under to look back at her, Sirin was gone. She squeezed with all she had, trying to milk Berne into giving her every drop of cum he had. The rhythmic clench of her pussy around his cock made her scream into the night as she felt him press as deep as possible inside her, his knot slipping inside with a pop as he roared.

For the next few blissful moments, Sirin's mind was blank, save for the wash of pleasure that radiated through her body. The heavy press of

---

2. For those who do not know, a knot is a swelling at the base of the phallus.

Berne's weight grounded her in her ecstasy; the only sounds she heard were the deep guttural noises of his release.

Afterward, Berne rolled onto his back so Sirin lay atop his chest, running her fingers through the white fur of his chest hair. She raised her head to meet his eyes and smiled. "Welcome home."

Underneath her, he returned to his normal size and cuddled her closer. His knot released as he changed and he moved his fingers to keep his release inside of her instead.

"I swear, a few more welcomes like that, and yeh won't be able to make me leave again. Or I suppose I could just take yeh with me." Berne yawned, nuzzling into her neck. "Don't suppose yeh fancy sleeping outdoors? I'm beat."

Sirin pretended to consider. "Well, at one point you *were* nice and cozy in your own bed, you *could* have stayed there." She stood up and loomed over him, already missing the feel of his fingers and his cock. She put on a stern face, smacking him on the outside of his ass. "Now get up, I want a ride. I'm freezing."

Berne growled and rolled onto his stomach, shifting into his bear as he did so. Sirin was still researching what exactly the lunula had done to allow for the change; it seemed most of his people had accepted it as a gift from the Lady and moved on. Lady save her from people who accepted the gifts and never questioned how or why. She *hoped* she might be able to figure it out enough to allow herself to change. But, even if not, Berne indicated their children should be able to.

Once he was completely shifted, Berne startled Sirin from her musings with a thick tongue between her thighs, lapping his release as it dripped out of her. She giggled and pushed his head away.

"Don't start that again, I'm exhausted. You can have more in the morning if you need." She turned to scoop up her nightgown, and climbed atop her mate's back. She gripped his thick fur around his neck and squealed with delight as he took off toward home at full speed. As her hair whipped around her, the forest sounds surrounding them, Sirin realized for the first time in her life, she was truly happy rather than simply content.

THANK YOU SO MUCH for reading A Polar Expedition! If you'd like to see some spicy art of Sirin and Berne and read a bonus epilogue that accompanies it, you can join Kass's Newsletter!

Reviews are extremely important for authors, especially indie authors. If you enjoyed this book, please leave a review on Amazon and/or your favorite review platform. Even short, 20 word reviews that are rambling (the only variety the author is capable of) are so, so helpful, so never be shy!

It only takes a taste...

THE RAKE
OR
THE ORCA WHO MET HIS MATCH
IN A SELKIE DESIRING REVENGE
BY:
KASS O'SHIRE

Lost in strange waters after a narrow escape from captivity, Elspeth the selkie is determined to find and free her brother. When she runs into an orca-shifter who mistakes her for lunch, one drop of his blood on her pelt binds her to him... forever.

Aegir is a notoriously talented shifter, playing pirates and playboys wherever his covert operations--or many lovers--take him. But when the selkie he rescued vanishes, he's plagued by memories of her... and a letter that spells out her doom. As they come together to rescue Elspeth's brother, both must navigate their traumas, a bond neither wanted, and growing feelings for each other. Can Elspeth learn to trust someone who wears a different face every day?

Kass O'Shire returns with more of your favorite cozy, spicy, monster romantasy and this time its a swashbuckling adventure that flips the traditional selkie tale on its head. As an interconnected standalone, it's the perfect place to dip your toes into the word of the Shades of Sanctuary, where the vibes are cozy, the heat is high, and the mates are monstrous. Grab your favorite drink, a cozy blanket, and preorder The Rake, Or The Orca Who Met His Match in a Selkie Desiring Revenge today!

Pre-order now on Amazon!

Also By Kass O'Shire

Catrin will get a second chance at love—with her brother's best friend—in book two of the Shades of Sanctuary.
Read it now! https://amzn.to/43vugXG

ON THE
CARE AND KEEPING OF
ORCS

Kass is a reluctant human living in America's own little Shire. Kass uses she/her pronouns and is both is demi and bi. Her writing focuses on body, sex, and equality positive stories with high heat levels and cozy vibes. She loves monster romance/paranormal romance, gas-lamp fantasy romance, historical romance, sci-fi romance (ok, all things romance), epic fantasy and space opera. In her free time, she reads a lot, bakes her pants off, and plays and DMs DnD and other tabletop and board games. She's married to a pretty great guy who is convinced he is Berne (he's not), has one awesome 13 year old son and has done two surrogacies for the most amazing couple.

To pay the bills, Kass is a data analyst in mental and behavioral health. As a result, she's extremely passionate about access to care for all folks. As you could probably guess from the footnotes, she's a HUGE nerd ;)

The best place to hear things before ANYONE is Kass's Patreon! There, even free members find out juicy bits before the public, and she's better at updating it than her newsletter. Paid patrons get free ARCS, access to spicy art, the enire backlog of her extras and epilogues, sneak peeks as to what is coming next, bi-annual mailings of goodies and even book boxes and merch! Sign up now to stay in touch! patreon.com/kassoshire

You can find Kass ALL THE PLACES via her Carrdhttps://kassoshire.carrd.co/(Generally patreon, discord and insta will get you the most up to date info!)

Acknowledgments

IN WHICH KASS IS
EXCEEDINGLY GRATEFUL FOR
THE MYRIAD INDIVIDUALS
THAT MADE THIS BOOK
POSSIBLE, KEPT HER SANE,
AND SUPPORTED IT'S
PUBLISHING

A village really raised this book baby from it's initial conception. I have more people to thank than I can possibly remember, but here are a few. Thank you beyond what I can possibly express to:

My friends, family, and coworkers: Y'all have put with a lot from me to see this book baby born, even if you never even read it, I appreciate your support.

Discord communities: GKS, FaRo, MonsterBait, Monster Fudgers, Beignets, Book Whores of Yore, Polycule Corner–I spend a LOT of time on Discord y'all and these communities have kept me sane when I was losing it, brought me joy when I needed it, found me more friends than I can count and lifelong connections for which I am forever grateful. I am so indebted to the members of these communities for their beautiful spirits, hilarious memes, nsfw art, consistent motivation and unwavering support.

My DnD/tabletop groups: Thanks for letting me derail so many sessions talking about book stuff and the constant tentacle porn jokes. Most of you are convinced you inspired this book, sorry, not this time, but there's always next time.

The other author's in our community: Honestly, there are too many authors in our community that have been so exceedingly wonderful to me that I am not sure I could even begin to thank them appropriately. The author community, especially our little fantasy/monstery corner of the universe, is so ridiculously wonderful. Especially helpful have been: S.E. Wendel, S.L. Prater, Catrina Bell, Allegra Hall, Sabrina Day, Michelle Matteson, Wren K Morris, Freydis Moon, Ash Raven, Rhea Fox, D.J. Russo, Shoshanna Rain, Gisele Briseia, Cia Petrichor, Lisette Marshall, and so, so many others. Please read all of their books and give them the most love.

My alpha readers: Luiza, Kendra,Kaitlyn, Tegan, Erin, Mark, Jo, and Natasha–Y'all loved this book before it was even remotely done and I am forever grateful. Your encouragements and notes grew this book by three chapters and it is SO much better for it.

My beta readers: Melissa E, Tori C and Melissa H–When I was worried if I had made enough changes, if I had grown this book in the ways it needed to, you reassured me and showed me to the little places it needed to stretch some more. You have been constant cheerleaders, and I can't tell how much your support buoyed me when I was feeling low.

My sensitivity readers: Pearly, Azalea Crowley, Stephanie, Darling, Sophia, Jackie—Thank you for sharing your culture with me. It was so special to me growing up and representing even a small part of Filipino culture through Sirin has been an honor. This loving people have shaped who I am as a person, as a spouse and as a mother. Salamat forever. Don't worry, we aren't even begun being done with Sirin yet. Next book: Food!

My amazing artists: PhantomDame, FantasySpriteStudio, FoxofTwilight, Aliiwa, and Taylaedraws– I am convinced y'all have sold more of my books thank I have. The way you have brought Sirin and Berne to life has captivated me and so many others who have seen your work. You've communicated things about them, their spirit and their relationship so beautifully in ways that I simply cannot. Special shoutout to LupeSilverwind who barely knows I exist, but drew the picture that essentially put Berne in my head.

My ARC readers: As I write this, you are actively

pointing out typos to save my butt, tagging me in good reviews, letting me ignore some not so good ones, screaming at me in my dms and helping me hold it together. A post or message from on of you raises my spirits for hours or days and is more motivating than a post from me might be for a potential reader. Thank you for all you have done and will do for me and other authors.

Dru: Your pointed feedback really helped bring this book to the next level. You have a unique ability to see through the heart of an issue that spoke to the issues that were tickling at the back of my mind. I am so, so grateful.

Brittnee: Since alpha stages, you have stuck by me, inspired me, cried with me, helped me solve problems, and been just an amazing friend. I am so lucky you answered that initial post and that we have wormed our way into each other's lives. We've got this, bestie.

Meg: You do ridiculous amounts for our community at large and have for me personally. Your tireless support of indie authors is astounding and I can't imagine how many books are purchased because of your hard work. To top it off, you are a stellar friend M'fires.

Carolina: You whipped this book into shape and I'm so grateful for our hours spent drafting and chatting, putting our evil alter egos in jail

and squealing over each other's lives. You are a
constant inspiration and motivation for me.

Torri: You are the reason I will always tell people
to meet their internet friends. There is something
so powerful about being friends with someone
based on shared interests instead of proximity.
Thanks for listening to me blather for hours about
this book and all of the lore, can't wait to do it
some more! Thank you for laughter and tears, silly
boardgames and letting me steal your babies.

Ashley Bennet: Through mental health,
parenting, art, and bookish stuff, we have seen each
other through a lot and you've helped me find my
way in this scary uncertain new world. I am so
grateful for our check-ins, and it's so wonderful to
have a friend like you. We can do hard things, and
I am so lucky to call you my friend.

C.M. Nascosta: When I demanded, like the
whiny baby butt I am, a bear shifter book, because
I was sick of them being so "traditional family
values" you told me it would be a few years and
to write it myself. I've been quiet lately, because of
this dang book, but your book brought me into this
community, and your community, where I have
found some of the most important people in my
life. Your words of wisdom have guided me toward
good choices, your blunt assessments and fierce
advocacy on behalf of your baby authors is always
appreciated. Please disregard the fact that we are

close in age when I say: I want to grow up to be like you.

Bex: Thanks for not letting me publish "engorged member," you are the Bext. This book couldn't have gotten done and I wouldn't even be the same person without you. Our brainstorming sessions are some of my favorite activities, ever. You've dealt with me when I was at my worst and helped me figure out when I was at my best. I cannot possibly express how grateful I am to you, how much I owe you, and how deeply I care for you.

Chris: Thanks for all you do. 12/10 husband. Thanks for jumping feet first into the world of monsterfuckery with me. I love you more than I can possibly express and I'm literally so obsessed with you it's unreal. My biggest wish is that everyone could have a partner as loving, supportive and understanding as you. You taught me that real men can be just as good as book boyfriends.

Finally, you, my reader: Thank you for spending time with me, Sirin and Berne. I cannot express how magical it is to know that people might be enjoying my silly little world. If I provided you with a little bit of joy, comfort or coziness, I am incredibly grateful for the opportunity.